Diary of a Warrior Villager
Ru's Adventure Begins!
First Four Books

An Unofficial Minecraft Series

Skeleton Steve

www.SkeletonSteve.com

Copyright

"Diary of a Warrior Villager Set 1 – Ru's Adventure Begins"

"Diary of a Warrior Villager – Book 1"

"Diary of a Warrior Villager – Book 2"

"Diary of a Warrior Villager – Book 3"

"Diary of a Warrior Villager – Book 4"

Published in the United States of America by Lightbringer Media LLC, 2018

To join Skeleton Steve's free mailing list, for updates about new Minecraft Fanfiction titles:

www.SkeletonSteve.com

Table of Contents

Contents

Book Introduction by Skeleton Steve

*Love MINECRAFT? *****Over 60,000 words*** *of kid-friendly fun!***

This high-quality fan fiction fantasy diary book is for kids, teens, and nerdy grown-ups who love to read epic stories about their favorite game!

All FIRST FOUR "Warrior Villager" Minecraft Diary Books in ONE!!

Thank you to <u>all</u> of you who are buying and reading my books and helping me grow as a writer. I put many hours into writing and preparing this for you. I *love* Minecraft, and writing about it is almost as much fun as playing it. It's because of *you*, reader, that I'm able to keep writing these books for you and others to enjoy.

This book is dedicated to *you*. Enjoy!!

After you read this book, please take a minute to leave a simple review. I really appreciate the feedback from my readers, and love to read your reactions to my stories, good or bad. If you ever want to see your name/handle featured in one of my stories, leave a review and *tell me about it* in there! And if you ever want to ask me any questions, or tell me your idea for a cool Minecraft story, you can email me at steve@skeletonsteve.com.

Are you on my **Amazing Reader List**? Find out at the end of the book!

July the 12th, 2018

For those of you who love Ru the Warrior Villager and his friends and family, and like a good deal, enjoy this Box Set! This bundle includes the FIRST FOUR BOOKS of the Warrior Villager Series. If you'd

2

like to see me continue the adventures of Ru and his friends, please let me know in the review comments!

P.S. - Have you joined the Skeleton Steve Club and my Mailing List?? *Check online to learn how!*

You found one of my diaries!!

Some of these books are my own stories, and some are the tales of the friends I've made along the way. And a precious few of my books, like this one, are from my "Fan Series", which means that it's a book I worked on *together* with one of my fans! Make sure to let me *and the fan who helped* me know whether or not you liked our book!

This Bundle of Books is from the *SunnyStar12* Fan Series. It takes place on a Minecraft world, much like my own Diamodia, where Villagers and Minecraftians live on the wild frontier as warriors and traders working together.

What you are about to read is the *first box set* of diary entries from Ru the Villager, the son of a famous Blacksmith, who wants nothing more than to be a powerful warrior and pursue the art of sword fighting! The life of a Villager is supposed to be peaceful, so he starts off at odds with his family, who want him to stay away from swords and training, but it doesn't stay that way for long...

Be warned—this is an *epic book!* You're going to *care* about these characters. You'll be scared for them, feel good for them, and feel bad for them! It's my hope that you'll be *sucked up* into the story, and the adventure and danger will be so intense, you'll forget we started this journey with a *video game!*

So with that, dear reader, I present to you the tale of **Ru the Warrior Villager**, the first **Box Set**...

Book 1

Ru is a young villager who wants to be a WARRIOR!

He loves when traveling knights visit his family's blacksmith shop, and longs to be a warrior like them. In fact, Ru wants to be a warrior so badly that he practices in secret with his uncle's old sword, until he gets in trouble with his family! Villagers are a people of peaceful traders, and there's no room for violence in villager life!

But when the mobs around town suddenly become more aggressive for no apparent reason, and everything in the boy's life is turned upside down, will Ru really appreciate finally getting the chance to test his warrior skills?

Book 1, Chapter 1

Clang. Clang! CLANG!

The sound of the hammer hitting iron horseshoes rang in my head.

It seemed there was always *clanging* or *smiting* or the crackle of fire ringing in my ears...

"Ru! Put some more fuel on, the fire is not hot enough," my brother Brew shouted. He didn't pause in his hammering, beating the hot metal into the open oval shapes beloved by horses everywhere.

I sighed and let go of the bellows to heap some more fuel onto the flame, then picked up the bellows again.

"Only twenty-one more shoes, then we can start trading," he yelled cheerfully. "Your favorite thing, Ru!"

"That is SO not true..." I started to sputter, but stopped when I saw Brew's mischievous grin.

"I know ... you hate it as much as I do. But it's all part of..."

"...Being a *blacksmith*," we finished together.

"And a blacksmith's work is never done, as long as monsters can see the sun," I added.

"Lame, but true. Let's switch," he said, "My arm is getting tired."

Brew and I changed places, him picking up the work of fueling and running the bellows to fan the flame.

I picked up a lump of iron with the tongs and thrust it into the fire until it turned a hot glowing red. I loved the color and the fierceness of molten metal. It was angry. A lot like how I felt at having to do this stupid job.

With the hammer in my other hand, I began shaping the metal. The hammer was heavy and fell down to earth with a *swoosh*, which was satisfying.

As I beat the metal, turning it with the tongs, I created a little song in my head.

I ... *clang*...

hate ... *clang*...

Smithy ... *clang*...

Work ... *clang*...

I'd ... *clang*...

Rather ... *clang*...

Be out ... *clang*...

Fighting! ... *clang*...

But as long ... *clang*...

As I'm told ... *clang*...

I will continue ... *clang*...

Iron Smiting ... *clang*...

"Good rhythm there, Bro," Brew said. If only he could hear my little song! "You've got a lot of strength—more than me. Remember to keep swapping arms so you don't end up with a giant one and a puny stick..."

We finished up the work, swapping roles as we tired, and switching the tools from our left hand to our right and back again.

The Village would be full of tourists wanting to trade, and they always needed horseshoes and other armor.

The thing was, I wasn't allowed to make any of the cool things, like weapons. That privilege was reserved for my father, the head blacksmith in the village. Brew was apprenticing, since he was older than me, and still didn't get to make weapons, but he at least was learning about them. I felt terribly jealous.

I longed to be able to pick up a sword, one made with the finest balance so it was easy to swing, then chop off a zombie head or two...

But no, we villagers just had to run away, lock ourselves indoors and avoid any challenge. Boring! Where was the adventure, the fun? My anger turned to depression with nothing but endless days of making horseshoes on my horizon. The clanging continued.

Finally, our work was done, and we went into the house to have lunch.

"How did it go?" Mom asked, putting our plates on the table.

"Pretty good," Brew answered. "We're well stocked and ready. "

Mom looked at me rather worriedly. She never worried about Brew who loved—*and I mean loved*—the family business.

"You okay Honey?" Mom asked. She had noticed my glower.

In reply, I picked up a piece of bread and stuffed it into my mouth, then nodded. "Sure," I said with my mouth full.

"Don't talk with your mouth full," she said automatically. My tactic distracted her from probing for more, as I knew it would.

Brew winked at me, and chowed down on some mutton chops.

Then it was time to get ready to trade; to change into clean clothes, fill our inventory and head out into the village square. It was a beautiful day. Strangers from all over filled the market. I loved watching people, especially the knights.

There was one in particular I found fascinating. He wore full diamond armor, and you could tell he was a mighty warrior. He confidentially looked around at all of the villagers. There was no fear in his gaze, and he walked with great strides.

When the Diamond Knight stopped in front of the baker to purchase some food, he stood and sparkled in the sunlight...

My imagination sparkled too at the sight of him. What great monsters had he destroyed? Hordes of zombies, I bet, and creatures I'd heard about but never seen! Ones I'd never even heard of, perhaps! Had he been in *the mountain*, or deep down in the caves?

Brew nudged me. "Pst, Ru! He's coming over!"

The Diamond Knight strode over to us and stopped, looking down at us with piercing eyes through the slits of his helm.

"Blacksmiths?" he queried in a booming, commanding voice.

"Yes sir," Brew replied, after clearing his throat.

"May I see your weapons and horseshoes, if you don't mind...?" He grinned, suddenly becoming human, and his strong white teeth flashed. "I am *always* in need of weapons."

Brew starting showing him our inventory, and I devoured every move the knight made.

I watched how he picked up our finest sword, checked to make sure no one was standing behind him, then swung it around in giant circles, testing its balance. I studied how he checked the blade to make sure that there were no faults, and whether or not the grip fit both hands...

"Feels good. I'll take it," he said. "Is your father the famous blacksmith *Cru?*"

"Yes, I am his son, Brew, and this is my little brother, Ru."

The Knight turned to assess me. I was taller than my brother, and strong from years of smithy work. I tried not to flinch or blush.

"You look like a *fighter*, Ru. Ever picked up a sword?"

Brew gasped in horror. "Sir, we villagers do not fight. Ever."

"A thousand apologies, lad. I did not mean to offend you. Here, let me take some more of your glorious items, and perhaps you will forgive an old and tired warrior."

We then began a huge and lively barter session with the Diamond Knight, and the warrior ended up leaving with three swords, loads of arrows, and all of our horseshoes.

"I have ten battle horses," he said, "and they are always throwing shoes. Good day!"

Ten horses?! *Blazes!*

After the Diamond Knight left, we returned home, whooping in excitement. We traded more in that day then we had in months!

"Boys, you did well," Dad said, clapping us on the shoulders and practically knocking us off our feet. "And you say this *Diamond Knight* liked my sword?" Dad rubbed his hands together gleefully.

"He loved it!" Brew beamed happily. "He said he'd be back for sure!"

"Molly, did you hear that?" Dad asked, lifting Mom up and spinning her around, her feet swinging in the air. She laughed uncomfortably, trying to get down. "Back for sure!"

"Cru, I'm so happy for you!" she replied. "Your weapons are magnificent, and you deserve it!"

After Dad put Mom back down and squeezed her a couple of times, he turned to me and said, *"One day* Ru, if you put your mind and heart to it, you can make weapons. And one day, maybe a sword of yours will see battle!"

Mom clapped her hands, "Wouldn't that be great, Ru?"

I gave her a kiss on the cheek. "Of course, Mom."

Of course, I didn't want to send a sword of my own making into battle. I wanted to *wield* it...

"In fact," Dad added, "Maybe it's time you started your apprenticeship? You can run bellows for Brew and I. How about it Son?"

There was a lot more whooping and hollering, then Dad said, "Now, let's go out for dinner to celebrate!" That showed how happy he was, because we never went out for dinner.

I pretended to be happy with the rest of them for the whole meal, laughing and joking, and acted excited about starting to make weapons, but inside, I was seething...

I didn't want to make weapons. I wanted to be a warrior! How could they not know me enough to understand that?!

That night, lying in bed and looking out the window at the stars, I decided that I would teach *myself* to fight...

I listened to the zombies roaming around, knocking on doors, and I thought about what it would be like to fight them, instead of just running away, or waiting until they turned into ash in the morning sun. Oh, to slice their heads off, or hammer them until they exploded! Such sweet thoughts...

Finally, I fell asleep, and dreamed about diamonds and gold armor and horses stomping their feet to the beat of the hammer, glowing with red hot fire...

The morning routine was a little different the next day, because it was the beginning of my new role. I ran the bellows and watched while my brother and Dad took scrap metal and beat it into pointy shapes.

"Now pay attention," my father told me, the sweat running down his face. "Listen to everything we say and watch our movements. You'll be amazed at how much you absorb."

It was the most boring thing in the world, but I pretended to be interested.

When we took a break, I activated my plan. In the back of the smithy was a big barn used to store our supplies and test the new weapons. (*If only I could test the weapons, but no—villagers did not do such things...*) I spent a couple of days designing a scarecrow figure, and kept it hidden behind some hay bales used for target practice. I pieced together some armor, and even drew a face. Mom was a painter, and I stole some of her green paint and made it look like a zombie. I named it Zillow. I liked to name things.

What I did next was a little terrible, and I knew that if I were to get caught, I'd be in huge trouble!

I 'borrowed' a sword from Dad's collection. It was a small one, and it was in the back of the shop underneath some other things, so I prayed that he wouldn't notice.

But I needed it—I needed to *hold a sword*. I had to...

Every chance I got after that, I went out and took a couple of *whacks* at Zillow, and I tried to figure out how to use that little sword. Most of the time, I'd do more sawing then slicing. It was easy to reattach Zillow's head when I needed to, or stuff more hay into the torso.

Days went by, and I started to get better. It was so much fun. But then, one day, something terrible happened. The worst thing I could imagine...

I got caught.

I was having a grand fight with Zillow. Dad and Brew were working on something in the shop, and Mom was in the garden. Zillow was being very aggressive, and taunting me with names. One of those times I thought I imagined Zillow yelling at me turned out to be a real voice—voices in the barn!

It's easy to admit now that I panicked. Instead of stopping my swing in mid-air as soon as I heard my dad's voice, and hiding until he went away, I jerked out the sword's blade, and chopped Zillow's head clean off! It went flying out from behind the hay, rolling and rolling until it stopped at my dad's feet, staring up at him blindly...

I popped my head out to see what had happened, and saw my Dad's face change from surprise to fury.

"What in the blazes is *this?!*" he yelled, picking up the head. When Dad said the word *blazes*, you knew you were in for it. "Ru. Do not move..."

Dad stomped toward my hiding place, and Brew followed miserably behind.

Looking down at Zillow and my little nest of weapons and armor, then seeing his own sword—which I was stupidly still holding in my hand—Dad silently fumed...

There were a million things I could have done—hidden the sword while he was stomping over, or run for the hills to name two. But I didn't do anything. I only stood there, frozen in fear.

"Oh, blazes..." I heard Brew whisper. My brother's words kind of popped me out of my stupor. I dropped the sword and ran for the hills. Well, not literally. I actually ran up into my bedroom, past Mom who was holding bunches of lettuce. I slammed the door, then stood there, shaking.

"What's going on?" I heard Mom say. There was a murmur of voices. Then silence. *That* was scarier than anything...

Book 1, Chapter 2

Nothing happened. I don't mean that I wasn't in trouble, but no one came to my room. No one pounded on the door. No one spoke coldly, or yelled.

It was the worst punishment I'd ever received, even worse than the time I'd let all the rabbits loose and they ate the garden.

Time passed, and it grew dark. There wasn't much to do in my room. Look out the window. Lie down on the bed. Look at the wood in the ceiling. Lie on the floor. Look out the window again.

I started to get hungry, and my mind started having conversations with my dad— trying to explain to him; wondering what he would say...

Eventually, I couldn't stand it and cracked the door open. The clink of dishes told me that it was dinner time. I couldn't stay up there forever, and besides, I smelled my favorite food: roast chicken.

Mom probably cooked it to lure me down. Or maybe I would get down there and I wouldn't get to eat any; I'd just have to sit there and watch them eat.

I tiptoed to the head of the stairs and peeped down.

They were all sitting at the table. My place was set, and I could just see the corner of my dad's sleeve.

I slid quietly into my wooden chair, careful not to let it scrape on the floor. I didn't look at anyone.

Brew kicked me under the table, which made me feel better. But no one spoke to me. When I finished eating, I peeped at my mom. Her eyes were red and it made me feel terrible.

Eventually, I slid back upstairs, wondering how long this silent treatment would last.

Why was it so terrible to want to be a hero? I felt so mixed up with guilt and anger. Why was I so different? I didn't know a single other villager who felt the way I did and wanted to be a warrior.

But it was ridiculous to make weapons and not be able to use them...

Night came and went, zombies growled and moaned, and I didn't sleep a wink.

The next morning, I went to breakfast, and Brew was the only one down there. He poured me a glass of milk and handed me some fresh bread.

"So Dad's really mad, then," I finally mentioned, trying to be as casual as I could.

"Eh ... you could say that." Brew's voice was flat. I know he was torn, since I was his little brother, and he loved his dad too.

"Sorry, Brew. I don't mean to put you in the middle."

Brew stopped eating and gave me a level look. "I know that. I know you've been crazy about fighting and adventures ever since you were little. Meeting the Diamond Knight stirred you up too, didn't it?"

"I can't help it. " I looked miserably down at my plate.

Brew patted me on the shoulder as he stood up. "Well, I'm sure things will end up okay. I'm not sure how, but something will happen. Let's go to work."

When I arrived at the smithy, Dad was there. "Go away," was all he said.

"But, Dad!"

"Go away." Then he turned his back.

Blazes! To be frozen out by my own father. It was agonizing! I went and found Mom.

"Mom?" I was a little hesitant to approach her, but surely she wouldn't cast out her little boy, right?

Right. Whew! As soon as Mom saw me, she leapt to her feet and grabbed me in a fierce hug. Normally I'd hug her for a few seconds, then break the hold. This time, however, I let her hug me as long as she wanted to.

"Let's have some tea," was all she said, and I picked up her gardening basket and followed her to the kitchen.

We didn't speak while she made tea, but it was a lot more comfortable than the meal last night. Moms are great, warm and cozy. Mine was better than great...

But then, she started a story. I rolled my eyes. She's great but not *perfect*. Mom's stories were LONG...

"When I met your father...." she began and it wasn't until the second mug of tea that she got to the meat of her tale.

"You're like your uncle, Ru, and it's painful for your dad to think of him."

I was astounded. "I have an *uncle?*"

"You *did*." She looked sad, and swirled her tea.

"What happened? Is he dead?" I just couldn't believe this. Why had no one ever mentioned to me that my dad had a brother?

After a terribly long—seemed like forever—pause, mom continued. "Your Uncle Bob was a lot like you, not content to be a peaceful villager and continue in the family business, which goes back *blah blah blah* ... but instead of thinking about things, being calm and logical, he was impulsive, and quick to anger. He also wanted to see more of life..."

"That *is* like me! What happened to him?"

Mom sighed. "He went off to fight in the *Skeleton Wars*, and never came back. Someone brought his sword back, along with his helmet. We don't even know where he'd gotten that stuff from..."

I had an awful thought. "The sword I've been training with—was that...?"

"Yes," Mom said. "It belonged to Bob, and that's all we have left of him. Your dad never spoke about your uncle again after he disappeared."

"Mom, how do I fix this?" I buried my head in my hands. If I had just listened and never started this training...! Curse my adventurous nature!

"I don't know, son, but time fixes everything, one way or another." She patted me on the shoulder, the same way as Brew did. "I'll speak to your father, and after a bit, we'll get you talking. Then we'll see."

Small comfort, but it helped.

Dad gradually warmed up to me. Actually, it only took two days, and we were acting as if everything was normal again.

But I wasn't feeling normal at all. If anything, I wanted to train more than ever! It was a burning urge that kept growing. And growing and growing. It was bigger than the Iron Golem that patrolled our village.

I would have to talk to him. Dad, not the Golem.

Courage is a very weird emotion. Standing in front of my father, while he sat gently engraving a piece he was working on, I trembled more at his gentleness then I would have if he'd been yelling. Anger can fuel you, I guess. If my Dad had yelled at me, I could have defended myself.

But I felt helpless and vulnerable approaching him now.

"Dad?"

He ignored me. I persisted.

"Dad!"

He sighed, and looked up. "I guess you're going to keep trying to talk to me, aren't you? Wait while I finish this..."

I waited, watching his big hands move with delicacy. Was he wondering about his brother, my uncle?

At last, he stopped, swiveled to face me, and put his hands on his thighs. "Now, what do you want to say to me?"

I swallowed, and said, "I know about Uncle Bob. I know I'm like him, but I can't help it. I have this urge inside me to do more than this..." I gestured around at all the iron and gold, helmets and knives. "Brew loves this work, but I don't."

Dad shook his head sharply, and said, "I'm sorry Ru, but I absolutely forbid you to train, fight, think of fighting, or dream about fighting. It is not right. We are peaceful, intelligent and kind people. It is our way to work hard and trade. Fighting will create more fighting. Fighting will get you killed."

"But we *make* weapons!" What kind hypocrisy was this? The anger kicked in. Good.

"We don't *use* them." He said this as if it made perfect sense.

Oh my blazes, I just didn't understand! "I don't know what I'm supposed to do...?"

"Forget it, Ru. Control it. Push that fire *far away*. Someday, you will have your own family, and then you'll understand."

"And what if I can't? What if I can't *push it away?*"

"You must. That's all I'm going to say." Dad stood, and put his arm around me. "You *must*," he repeated softly.

But I didn't see how I could.

Over the next few days, I did try. I took apart poor Zillow and put my training things away—except for the horseshoes. Every time we played the game as a family, I kept seeing zombies instead of posts. Ringing my shoes around their imaginary necks was a little satisfying...

I really wanted to use those heavy horseshoes on a real zombie, because for some reason, the zombies were getting worse. There were more of them, and they seemed faster too. All of the villagers were talking about it in nervous murmurs, and making sure that their doors were nice and secure.

It was weird, but since the zombies weren't literally getting stronger, they weren't really a problem. Yet.

All the same, I kept my eyes open, and I always carried a horseshoe, just in case.

It seems like something always happens when you get into a pattern that's comfortable. Let your guard down, and life just slaps you in the face! Then you wake up.

This particular slap came in the form of another visiting knight—not the Diamond Knight. This warrior was gold, but a particular blackened gold. I'd never seen anything like it.

The Blackened Knight was there at the market, and actually came in search of *us*.

His eyes were cold, and black like his armor.

"You're the blacksmith's boys, aren't you?" he asked. His voice matched his eyes.

Brew answered with some pride, "Yes, we are."

"You have a reputation for spectacular swords. Can I see them?"

While Brew showed the dark warrior our inventory, I checked out the Blackened Knight's armor. He was very different than—as I privately called him—our *DK*. The Diamond Knight seemed kind and noble, someone to trust. This fellow seemed menacing. I looked over at his horses, and their eyes were shuttered. You can tell a lot about a person by their horses.

Each horse was jet black, all the same size, all wearing the same armor as the knight. Even the attendants were dressed in the same blackened gold color. Overall, the knight and his troop waw very imposing ... or menacing.

I wandered over casually and pretended to look at the horse, but I was really interested in the armor. What kind of metal was that? Perhaps gold that had been smudged dark with ash? Couldn't be ash—it had a little *shimmer*...

A voice startled me. "Young blacksmith, what do you think of our armor?" The voice had a particular hissing quality, and a shiver ran down my spine. "It's very *special*."

"Wow," I said as the Blackened Knight walked up behind me. "It's amazing. I've never seen that kind of metal before.

What's it made from?" I looked at the dark warrior. For some reason, he reminded me of a snake with flat eyes and skin that was slightly slimy.

"It's a secret," he replied.

I put a hand out to touch it, and he pulled me back.

"Don't touch," he added.

Even though I felt a little flush of anger at that, I didn't give the knight a hard time. I just shrugged, and went back over to stand next to Brew.

My brother had just finished with the knight, and was clearly excited, but trying not to show it.

Once the Blackened Knight and his company was gone, Brew smiled broadly. "Come on, let's go," he said, and headed for home at a trot. I followed, but turned for one more look. Part of me felt awakened and brilliantly alert; tingling, and feeling danger and power.

The Blackened Knight was standing further away in the market, watching us leave.

Weird.

Book 1, Chapter 3

Dad was really excited again. "We're getting a reputation. If we keep this up, we'll be the most renowned smithy in all of the nearby villages!

Brew's eyes sparkled, and he said, "And Sir Darwym said that he wants us to make him a special sword sometime. He'll bring the metal for us. It's only found in his region."

Dad nudged me. "*That's* a little interesting, isn't it?"

"I can truthfully say that it is very interesting." I was telling the truth, too, though I was a lot more interested in the Blackened Knight and his odd horses than making a stupid sword.

The pleased look on Dad's face made me a tiny bit ashamed, since things had been going pretty well. But at least I was behaving myself now!

Every evening for a while now, Brew had been going out to the shop to practice his skills with left over pieces. I couldn't bring myself to join him—that was pushing my attempt to force interest in blacksmithing too far. But Brew was into it, and Dad was delighted.

Tonight, however, since things were very quiet in town and I was a bit on edge from meeting those weird people, I decided to go out and see what Brew was up to.

It was pretty safe—the shop was only twenty feet or so away out the back door of the house, and we had a good fence built around the yard to keep the Z's out. Torches lit the path, and I could see light shining from the shop windows up ahead. From our yard, you could see the fields shine in the moonlight...

I looked around sharply as I walked across the yard. The feeling of danger from this afternoon hadn't left me. And it was too quiet. I expected to hear clanging or metal scraping, but the only sounds from around me were the crickets and some kind of ... scraping.

Once I reached the shop door, which we usually left open, I walked in. "Brew?" I called out. Maybe he was in the storage room...

"Ru! Don't come in. Run! *Get outta here!*" His voice was unlike I'd ever heard it, almost a shaky scream!

My heart jumped into my throat. Danger! And of course, instead of running away, I ran *in* ... then I stopped dead in my tracks when I saw what was going on.

A giant spider had Brew trapped in a corner! Brew was avoiding its fangs using a shield from the shop inventory, but the spider was determined to get at him, and hissed furiously!

That spider was so big, it didn't even need to rear up on its spiky legs to try to bite Brew's head off. It stood on six legs and punched the shield down on top of Brew with its front claws, then tried to pry it off as Brew struggled beneath...

I had to do something!

Looking around wildly for something to help, I was dismayed that there was nothing around my but little bolts and things. Still, I grabbed whatever I could get hold of, and threw blacksmith bolts and other junk as hard as I could at the spider!

Pieces of metal rained down on its head, and it turned towards me in irritation.

Its eyes glowed, and its fanged clicked together...

Uh oh. Now what?

Ah ... I reached into my inventory and pulled out a *horseshoe* that I always had me, and with all of my might, I flung it at the head of the beast, yelling "DUCK" to Brew in case I missed!

My aim was true, and it hit the spider right in the middle of the forehead, killing it.

"Bam!," I shouted. "Take *that* you blazing spider!"

The huge creature rolled over on its back, and its legs curled up.

Brew slowly lowered the shield, stood, and leaned it up against the wall with a shaky smile. He was trembling like a leaf! My brother walked over to me, making a wide circle around the ball of spider legs on the floor, and we both stood there, staring at it...

Finally he said, "Is it dead?" I picked up a stick near the furnace—*oh yeah*, I could have used *that!*—and poked it. The spider disintegrated, leaving behind nothing but a single, red eyeball...

"Eww..." Brew said, but I picked up the grisly body part carefully, and put it into my inventory. You never know when something's valuable!

"Here, sit down," I said, leading my brother over to the bench. "Did it bite you? Tell me what happened!"

Brew sat down with a *plonk*. "I don't know. I was putting my things away for the night, and turned around, and there it was! It just started attacking me, out of nowhere. If that shield hadn't been leaning against the wall there, I would have been *spider food*..."

"Spiders don't attack villagers. They attack tourists, sure, but they've always left *us* alone. What the heck is going on?"

"Yeah, the *zombs* are different too," Brew replied. He stood and hugged me. "Thanks, Ru! You saved my life. You're a hero. You saved me from that crazy spider with a horseshoe. I'm sorry I've been giving you a hard time about fighting. I think you're right. You *should* be a fighter, you were amazing!"

I hugged him back. "Well, I've been practicing, but don't tell Dad. He'd just get mad even though I did ... um ... save your life or whatever..."

"Right, he would. But I'll tell him about the spider—I'll just say that it went away. He'll have to warn everyone. Let's get home!"

As we returned to the house, I thought that I saw a dark movement in the shadows, but I could have been mistaken—I was so full of energy.

Brew came to my room after mom and dad went to bed. He spoke quietly. "I just wanted to give you something I've been working on..."

"What is it?"

My brother pulled out a beautiful iron sword, and handed it to me. It gleamed in my candlelight. "I want you to have it. I was going to give it to Dad, but you saved my life today."

I took the blade, and it sat perfectly in my hand...

It had a smooth, metal sword, with fine etching around the hilt and handle. The design wasn't perfect, but the blade was straight, and I was overwhelmed with graciousness.

"Holy Knight!" I exclaimed, then contained myself and quieted down. "A sword! I'll treasure it forever, Brew! Thank you!" And I did keep that sword, throughout the rest of my adventurous life. This special sword would always stay with me...

That night, when I looked out the window, the whole world seemed to glow.

All of those months—years—of discouragement and stuffing my feelings down had been exploded out of existence with the killing of that spider! I was a hero! I had saved my brother! I had an awesome sword hidden under my bed. It didn't matter if I had to pretend to like being a smithy now. In fact, there were parts of it I really enjoyed. Maybe I would learn to make awesome weapons, and work out a way to use them.

The fact that I'd killed something evil didn't bother me at all. I was glad, and would kill a thousand more! Line 'em up!

That night, I slept like a baby, and woke up eager for the next day.

It was another trading day, and this time I was much more interested in who was buying what. Why would one knight buy one type of sword and not another? Hmm...

I even tried haggling a little, and was surprised to see that I was good at it. One soldier came up, offering iron in exchange for a good sword, and I was able to talk him into not only buying the blade, but also coming up with more iron and gold for a new breastplate, too!

The village had a lot of visitors every week. People came from miles around to trade with us, and sometimes stayed for many days. Some villagers had nice houses that tourists would pay to stay in, or farms which also offered cooked meals. Knights would bring their apprentices and horses to train them on the flat fields around the village. Every once in a while, there'd be a race, or a village feast.

So I was curious if the Darkened Knight, Sir Darwym, had set up camp. Since trading had gone so well and we were done for the day, I thought I'd take a walk to the other side of the Village to see.

I passed the shops and homes, smiling and waving. I knew everyone, since I had been born and raised here, and everyone else had been born and raised here, too.

A few times on my path, I ran into someone who stopped me to chat, and we had a short conversation about the weather or some such thing. The sun was shining, and it was a beautiful day.

I hadn't visited the other side of the Village and the *Knight Camps* for a while. For as several days now, ever since meeting the Diamond Knight, I'd been thirsty to watch their training and lifestyle, but lately, thinking about my family fight about my warrior hobby, the place just gave me a sour stomach.

There were three camps: a small one with just a few people, and two good size groups. The one I was looking for was on its own a little way out in the field.

I wandered over, meandering through the warriors and their tents. Most of the non-villager people there were friendly, or just focused on whatever they were doing. Some waved, and one guy who was shining his armor chatted with me a bit. But when I arrived at the Darwym Camp, very few people even looked at me. It felt chilly there, despite the sunshine.

There was metal clanging on metal, and I followed the sound. It sounded like fighting!

I weaved my way past tents and small campfires. Everything was neat, and all of the tents were black. There were a few flags, red with a flame and crescent moon...

Then, one big soldier stepped out from behind a tent and barked at me. "What are you doing here?" He took a menacing step in my direction, and I automatically felt for the horseshoe in my pocket...

Yikes! And weird!

I didn't want to say that I was *poking around* so I said, "I'm the son of Cru the Blacksmith, and I was checking to see if you needed anything."

Good story! I smiled.

"I remember you." I suddenly heard a voice behind me. Oh it was Ssslithery, as I nick-named the snake-like man—the Blackened Knight. The soldier brute before me evaporated.

"I remember you, as well," I replied pleasantly, unclenching my hand. "Do you need any weapons or armor or anything?"

"I don't think so. We purchased what we needed the other day, as I recall." He eyeballed me.

Was it my imagination, or did Ssslithery seem suspicious? Oh dear, what to do now?

"Um, we've been having some trouble in the Village with zombies and spiders. Have the mobs around here been bothering you too?"

Ssslithery laughed, and my nickname for him was prefect. "Not at all. It's been very peaceful, and as you can see, we're well protected."

A particularly loud clang and yelp distracted me, and the Blackened Knight followed the direction of my gaze with his own. "You might be interested to see our training, Ru. Come with me."

Blazes, I thought. He remembered my name!

The Blackened Knight led me to a fighting arena, where we stood, silently watching.

Three men, in the same blackened gold armor I was so fascinated by, surrounded a small man dressed only in cloth. They all had swords...

One man took a swing at the man in the center, who swung around to deflect the blow, while the other pricked him in the backside with the point of his sword.

Center man twirled around frantically to defend his flank, then, the third man smacked him with the flat of the blade.

It didn't look like a game. The three bullies had cruel smiles, like they were enjoying hurting him too much, and the center man looked desperate...

The lone defender lunged at the bully closest to me with his full weight, trying to knock one of his three attackers off of his feet.

Success! The other two, however, didn't seem to like the result...

I couldn't watch. It wasn't sporting or practical—this was a beating.

As I looked away, I suddenly saw a small piece of metal go flying towards me, landing near my foot in the grass. I turned to go, pretended to stumble, and managed to pick it up on the sly.

Was it some of that weird, blackened gold metal?

"Seen enough?" Ssslithery asked, walking with me back through the camp. "We are one of the most powerful armies in the world! I'll tell you what—why don't you bring some more items tomorrow, and we'll take a look? I appreciate someone who is interested in fighting..."

"Okay."

The Blackened Knight watched me leave, perhaps to make sure that I didn't take any detours. I was almost expecting an arrow in the back, and it wasn't until I stepped into the Village Square that I stopped to look at the sliver of metal I had picked up from the ground.

It was a tiny chip of armor, laying like a black worm in my hand...

Book 1, Chapter 4

Later, I showed the mysterious shard of metal to Brew, and told him about my little adventure in the Blackened Knight's camp. He was unimpressed.

"So what? Fighters are mean and weird." he said, then added hastily, "*some* fighters, anyway. You're amazing..."

After seeing what I saw that afternoon, I had to agree with him—at least about the knights. I rolled my eyes about the praise.

Brew punched me lightly on the shoulder. "But nice work getting us some new business. I never thought of going to the Knight Camps to trade. You're smart."

I was a little pleased with the idea myself, even if the concept of going there for business was just a story to save my skin. We could make a regular practice of trading by going straight to the customers—in a quiet way at least, so that the other villagers didn't get the same idea.

It grew dark outside, and my brother and I made sure that everything was locked up tight.

At dinner, Brew and I brought up the new idea, and both Mom and Dad were both delighted. The encouragement felt really good, and Mom said, "Well, I'm glad I made roast chicken and potatoes."

During our fruit course, Dad brought up the subject of the weird behavior of the mobs in the area. There had been a big village meeting that afternoon. I could remember hearing the meeting bell earlier, but had simply ignored it at the time. Only the adults go to those meetings.

"The Elders are getting concerned," Dad said, "and they recommend that we travel in groups at night, and avoid tight spaces. In fact, several other people were threatened by spiders like you were Brew, but no one was outright attacked. We need to be careful—that big spider might come back!"

Brew and I looked at each other knowingly. We knew better.

Dad continued. "Another thing we noticed was that our Iron Golems seem a bit sluggish. But no one knows what to do, or what's causing the problem. The Librarian is looking into it and—"

He was interrupted by a loud zombie moaning.

"They're getting bold," Mom said, "and there seem to be more of them. I'm worried Cru..."

Dad finished his food and took his plate over to the sink. "In the morning, let's reinforce our fences, and make sure there aren't any holes, okay?"

A shadow passed by the window, then another. We could hear the undead banging on our neighbor's door. Mom stood by the sink, withdrawn, and Dad put his arm around her.

"It's okay, Molly. They can't get in here."

But Dad spoke too soon. The kitchen door, opening onto the street, was suddenly hit with a furious force! The fist bashed the door so hard, it started to splinter and break. Growling and moaning filled the room...

Mom screamed as a group of zombies burst into the kitchen!

"Quick, out the back door to the shop!" Dad shouted, running to us and pushing us out of the way.

A zombie tried to get around the table, and Brew pushed the chair in front of it. Mom picked up a frying pan and whacked one in the head with it, but it didn't seem to do any good. Dad stepped in front of Mom to protect her, holding one chair in midair to block the mob, then shouted again, "Go—now *RUN!*"

Brew and I grabbed anything we could throw, and started pelting the zombies: dishes, paintings, food. We trapped one with the heavy table, and another under a bookcase. It seemed like there were hundreds of them! They just kept coming in!

I rushed to the stairway to get the sword Ru forged for me from upstairs, but the way was blocked. The kitchen entrance, with the front door off of its hinges, was also blocked—choked with the writhing bodies of the undead. The door to the basement had a very large and angry zombie right in front of it. There was only one way out: the back door.

Brew grabbed my arm and pulled me. He stuck his head outside, and I half expected something to bite it off. But then he gave a quick look back, and said, "It's clear, come on!"

Dad yelled, "Go, we're right behind you!"

Brew and I ran outside toward the shop, where there'd be weapons and safety...

I turned back to help Mom, horrified by what I saw...

There was nothing but a sea of zombies in the house, and my parents were in the middle of it!

"Grab weapons!" I screamed, and picked up a shovel and started beating one zombie with it.

Brew ran like the wind into the shop, then came back with swords and shields.

We fought our way back into the house—back to Mom and Dad—killing zombies however we could! It wasn't pretty or elegant, and I didn't care. Mom and Dad were in there, and I had to save them, just like I saved my brother!

Brew used his shield to protect us, and I stabbed and hacked at one zombie after another until they dropped before us. Finally, we cut our way back into the kitchen. The crowd of moaning undead was thinning, and at least no more zombies were coming in from the street.

Mom and Dad were huddled together in a corner, using the table as a barrier. Thank goodness they were safe!

"Mom! Dad!" I shouted over the noise of the fight. "We're coming! Hold on!"

I killed the last zombie with a mighty war cry, while Brew ran out to check the street. Before checking on our parents, I rushed up stairs and made sure that no zombies were lingering on the second floor. The coast was clear.

When I made it back downstairs, I saw Brew running back in from the street.

"I don't see any more," my brother said. "I think we got them all."

"Mom, Dad," I said, breathing hard and looking at the hiding place of the dining table leaning up against the corner, "come on out. It's safe!" When they didn't immediately respond, I ran over and lifted the table off of them, shoving it out of the way. Brew gave me a hand.

But when we turned to our parents, there was Dad, with his big arms wrapped around Mom, dressed in her pretty apron, with dark green faces and dead eyes...

They ... were zombies!

Horrified...

Shocked...

Devastated.

None of those words even hinted at the emotions I felt boiling through me.

In fact, a whole mess of thoughts and emotions punched me in the gut, and the room started to spin and go dark.

Brew, his face white and streaked with tears, shook me.

"Snap out of it, Ru! Look out!"

Mom—my mother—was reaching for me with outstretched arms; not to hug me, but to *grab me*, so that she could bite me with her mouth opened wide...

"Quick—the table!" Brew shouted, and as quickly as we could, we pushed the table back to trap them in the corner again. This worked for a few minutes, until Dad's *super smithy strength* started shoving the table back toward us.

"Oh, *blazes!*" I cried, pushing the table back against zombie-Dad with all my strength. "What are we going to do? We can't hurt them!"

"Can you hold them?" Brew asked frantically. When I grunted *yes*, for I was using all my strength and body weight to keep the table in place, he ran over to the basement door, and started moving the kitchen and dining room furniture around it.

"Hurry!" I cried.

My eyes were closed. I couldn't look at my parents, so I was hoping that Brew was doing something clever to help...

"One Sec..." *CRASH*. "Almost..." *BANG*. "Hang on..." *SCREECH*. "Ready!"

I opened my eyes and turned to look. Brew had moved everything out of the way, and made a sort of path to the basement door, which was wide open. He had stacked things on either side to sort of *herd* my parents into the doorway, leading down...

"We'll trap them in here!" Brew exclaimed. "I'll have to draw them in, and squeeze out of the basement window before they can eat me!"

I shook my head. "What if they catch you, Brew?"

"Then lock us *all* in, and get some help." My brother looked into my eyes, and I saw a calmness come over him. The calm, strong older brother. Pure determination. He was awesome...

"Okay. Okay."

I prepared myself to move the table aside and jump out of the way. Brew stood in the basement doorway, ready to *book it*.

As I began to move, I paused, and shouted, "Wait, is the basement window unlocked?"

Brew's face paled. "Hold them. I'll check," he said, and disappeared. I could hear his feet pounding down the stairs over the growling groan of my dad. It felt like forever, but a few seconds later, my brother was back.

"Ready," he said.

We nodded to each other.

Years of working as a team saved us. If we hadn't had the ingrained harmony, this story would ended there. Instead, I pulled the table out, ducked underneath it at the same moment as Brew jumped up and down while yelling to distract Mom and Dad.

Our zombified parents moved toward him, and I watched from behind the table as they shuffled away—claws outstretched and mouths gaping—to devour their oldest child.

"Come and get me, Mom! Dad, I broke your chisel! I drank all the milk!" Absurd things were pouring out of Brew. I didn't think he needed to irritate them— just breathing was motivation enough to make zombies chase you. But I didn't say anything. My brother was doing great.

As soon as they were halfway down the stairs, I snuck up behind them to the door, and shut it. Luckily it opened outward into the kitchen, so I could barricade it, and it wouldn't be able to be opened from the inside...

I just hoped that Brew got out in time. As I was piling things up in front of the door, he finally came panting in from the back door. Brew had also swung by the shop, and picked up hammers and nails.

"No problems," he said. "Now let's lock them in."

We hammered the basement door shut, then ran outside to the basement window. Dad was trying to help Mom up onto a table so that she could reach it.

"How sweet..." I said, eliciting a smirk from my brother.

We hammered the window shut too, putting boards over it so that the sun wouldn't set our parents on fire. At least they would be safe for the moment...

I leaned my head against the boards to listen before I put the last nail in.

"Mom, Dad, I'm sorry I couldn't protect you," I whispered. "I'll do whatever I need to do to save you..."

It was an *Oath* made in a split second, but no Knight's Oath had been more fiercely sworn. I would save my parents, or die trying.

Probably die trying, I thought.

If at first you don't succeed, you die...

Brew said, gently, "Come on. We'd better fix the front door and check on the neighbors. I heard other people screaming, too." He headed back to the kitchen after putting hand on my shoulder.

"Yeah, okay," I said, following. I was felt relieved that we were at least doing *something*, and that moment of determination was powerful. I just couldn't think about Mom and Dad for now.

But this time, before we went to check on our friends, I made sure to grab my sword. And some horseshoes.

Book 1, Chapter 5

It was a long and awful night. Three other houses on our street were broken into by zombies while Brew and I were hacking and slashing our way back to Mom and Dad. Most of our neighbors were able to run and hide, but two of them had also *turned*.

Brew and I managed to lock them into rooms as well, and one villager—a girl—was outright *missing*.

Blazes—what if she had turned, and I'd killed her trying to save Mom and Dad, thinking that she was just another normal zombie?!

My brother and I were careful not to kill any more zombies after that—we just captured them, just in case it was someone we knew. Another batch came down the street. I looked at each zombie face carefully. It was interesting that, although they looked almost identical, some of the person they were before still remained.

"I've heard stories that they can be changed back; that they can be alive again," Brew said as he held off one zombie with his shield. It looked a little like the baker from down the block...

"Me too." I also used a shield now, so that we didn't hurt them, but I had my sword ready. I always thought that the stories villagers turning into zombies and then turning back alive again were just tall tales that parents tell their kids, but maybe there was some truth in it. There had to be! Otherwise, what would we do with Mom and Dad?

After Brew and I finishing locking up the rest of the zombies on the block, we started searching for the missing girl. Other neighbors joined in, until we found her, safe and sound, hiding in a chicken coup.

The rest of the night, Brew and I went around the village to help, while people barricaded their homes. We had to get all of the remaining zombies indoors before the sun came out.

By dawn, everyone was accounted for, and no one's family would be living torches running around screaming. It seemed that the zombies quieted down during the day too, which was a relief, thank goodness!

The Village meeting bell rang at noon. There was no way I was going to miss this one.

When I walked toward the square, instead of seeing the beautiful shops and smiling people I was used to, everything was shuttered and quiet. Flowers were trampled; fences broken. I don't remember even hearing any birds. The Village looked like a completely different place.

The Village Elder stood in the center of the square to speak. For the first time in his life, his clothes were rumpled, and his glasses were broken and held together with string.

"Attention! Attention!" he exclaimed. "A terrible tragedy has befallen us—a vicious and surprising attack in the night from the zombies that come from the forests around us! We must reinforce our Village before the sun sets again! For some reason, the zombies have attacked us with greater strength and ferocity than they normally show, and we Elders believe that they may come back..."

Everyone nodded at his obvious statement.

The Elder continued. "I have taken the further step on the behalf of the Village, of asking outside forces for additional help. Sir Darwym?"

The Blackened Knight stepped out into the center. Two of his largest soldiers towered on either side of him, hovering slightly behind.

Great, I thought, narrowing my eyes. This won't be good at all...

If anything, the three warriors looked colder and crueler in the warm sunlight than anything I'd ever seen.

Ssslithery took a long breath, and addressed the crowd.

"I understand you've had some problems with creatures." His voice was controlled and each word was slightly clipped. "I have agreed, in the interest of public decency, to leave two of my strongest soldiers here to help protect your Village."

There was a murmur of mixed reactions from the crowd.

The Blackened Knight continued. "We are moving on this week, but my men will stay to provide protection for as long as you need them."

"What's it going to *cost* us?" someone shouted out.

The Elder cleared his throat and spoke up. "The Elders have agreed that a small percentage of all our trades will be set aside for Sir Darwym, as long as we need his services." There was a gasp of outrage, and the Elder continued, hands held up in surrender. "I didn't know what else to do!"

Brew nudged me and whispered. "We could learn to *fight*." A man next to us heard, and looked horrified at the thought. The peaceful nature of a *Villager* was strongly ingrained, wasn't it?

I whispered back to Brew. "If we had more time, we could find some Villagers who were willing to learn to defend themselves and their families. But we need help *now*."

He nodded.

As much as I hated to admit it, we needed those stinking brutes.

And the smirk on Sir Darwym's face said that he knew it too.

After the official meeting, everyone but the Elders stayed, pretending to be busy so that we could all have the real meeting—to make a plan among the producers and traders of the town. Once the coast was clear, Betsy the Baker's wife passed out muffins and coffee. I sat cross-legged on the cobblestone, the coolness pleasant to my tired muscles.

The Librarian took a bite of muffin, then sighed in appreciation, then a sip of coffee, and another bite. Everyone relaxed and took a few moments to settle down.

Farmer Brown finally said to the air, "Did you notice how no one said anything about our families, or rebuilding?"

"Right," said the Butcher. "We'll have to take care of it ourselves."

"As always," a woman's voice quipped, and we all laughed a little.

She was right. It was up to us.

The Librarian put down his cup. "Okay, the way I see it, is we have a few immediate tasks. One, no matter who is 'protecting' us—and I doubt those two guards are going to do anything but want to be fed—" He paused for chuckles, then, "We need to rebuild. How can we strengthen our homes?"

"We've lots of iron scraps," said Joe, "We can make our doors out of iron instead of wood."

"Great idea, Joe. You get a group together, and get started this afternoon. What about the fences?"

"What about not just having *outside* fences, but fences on the end of the blocks, with gates?" That was from Carpenter Gryt. His tunic was torn, and although he looked tired, he did not look beaten.

"Sure, that will help a lot. Gryt, you're in charge of that one." The Librarian, true to his nature, had opened a book and was busy taking notes.

"Okay, now problem number two. First, more coffee, Betsy, please?" She poured him a second cup, and he breathed in its aroma in appreciation. "Ah, now number two: Spiders. They've been threatening us, and we should be prepared in case they attack. Fences won't keep them out."

Brew gave me a hard look.

It was time.

"Um," I spoke up. Everyone stared at me. "One actually attacked Brew the other day. It really wanted to kill him..."

"What happened?" Betsy gasped.

I was on the spot. Hopefully the Villagers wouldn't hate me.

"Well, I killed it with a horseshoe," I said as fast as I could, then closed my eyes, ready for the wrath. I prepared myself for a lecture about Villagers not fighting back. We were a peaceful people that existed by trading. That's what iron golems were—

But the Librarian just nodded thoughtfully. "You've got lots of those, don't you? And we're all pretty good at playing games and hitting targets! Why don't you boys make sure everyone's got a couple of horseshoes on them?"

Brew and I were astounded. I'm sure, looking back on that moment, that my jaw actually dropped.

"Really?" Brew asked. "We can do that..."

The Librarian chuckled. I felt like he read me like a book, and the man cast me a look that said, *I'm peaceful, not stupid*.

Betsy said, "I'll rip their legs off if I have to! Disgusting things."

I suddenly *loved* this Village!

"Task three," the Librarian said. "Something must be causing this increase in mob attacks. Maybe it's natural, or maybe not. But information is critical and knowledge is power. I'll be in charge of that one." He looked up toward the mountain in the distance, and I wondered what he was thinking. "But the most important immediate task: our families who were turned. We've got to turn them *back*, or, put them out of their misery." The Librarian looked at each person, full in the eyes, not deflating the issue. "Any ideas?"

I spoke up again. What was I becoming?

"Remember those old stories about restoring zombies back to normal? What about that?"

"Just tall tales, as far as I know," the Librarian replied, but he looked thoughtful away.

"Is there any information in the library?" Joe asked. "I remember those stories. My grandfather used to say that *his* grandfather was a zombie once."

The Librarian shook his head. "I've read every book, every letter, and every word in there. If it's true, and there is a way to restore the undead, then we just don't have the information in this Village."

Brew spoke up. "What about another village? Another Library?"

The Librarian stroked his chin, scanning the horizon. "There is a village over the mountains. The Librarian who lives there is *legendary*, and I know that he collects every book he can get his hands on! He and I write back and forth," he added modestly.

"Well it's worth a shot," said the Butcher, and several people agreed with him.

"But there is a problem with that," the Librarian said. "It generally takes weeks for our messages to get back and forth—"

"We can't wait weeks!" the girl who sold flowers sobbed. "My brother is locked in the kitchen. I can't even get into my house, and who knows how long he'll last?"

People murmured and cried, comforting the girl. The Librarian stared at the mountain range in the distance. The carpenter and butcher started arguing. Betsy started talking about her missing husband to anyone who was listening.

I spoke without thinking. "I'll go." When I didn't catch anyone's attention, I spoke up, repeating myself with my most booming, commanding voice. "I'll go!"

Everyone quieted down, and I realized how much I'd sounded like my father.

"I'll go with you," Brew said loyally.

"No," I replied, with everyone's eyes on me. I turned to Brew. "I'll go by myself—it'll be faster." When I spoke the words, I knew I had to do it. "You need to stay here and take care of Mom and Dad, and help the Village. I have a good chance of getting there and getting back alive—I'm not afraid to fight."

And it was true. After last night, I wasn't afraid—at least I had no fear or fighting or people knowing about my love of it anymore. I was indeed scared—terrified, in fact—of losing my parents, and failing. I didn't say anything about that, though.

No one argued.

No one tried to talk me out of it.

And even though I wanted to start away on the journey that very minute, I waited until the next morning, so that I was rested and prepared. With my sword and horseshoes packed, I enjoyed the rest of my time with my brother before strapping on my pack. For good measure, I took the spider eye and blackened metal shard along as well.

The whole village saw me off, bringing me whatever they had that might be useful for my journey—bread, string, tools. The Librarian even gave me a map and a message for his friend.

"Lou will help you, if anyone can," he said. "Good Luck, young Ru..."

"Thank you all. I'll do my best, and I'll be back with the cure as soon as I can."

I returned to Brew, who was standing on our doorway with tears in his eyes. He eyed the fantastic iron sword he forged for me, which was hanging at my waist.

"Be careful, Ru," he said, clapping a hand on my shoulder, trying not to cry. "I love you, Bro..."

I wiped the tears from my eyes before they fell, and steeled myself to turn away from my home.

"I will. You be careful, too. Take care of mom and dad. I love you, too, Brew."

With that, I gave Brew a fierce hug, then strode off into the wilds...

Book 2

The Journey of Ru

Bound and determined to find the fabled restoration technique to turn his zombie parents (and other afflicted villagers) back into living people again, Ru sets off, alone, on a great journey. The Warrior Villager is traveling to a distant village where a legendary librarian has a collection of knowledge so vast that he must have the secrets of the cure!

But how will a young villager who's never left his home before be able to endure the struggles along with way? How will he avoid getting lost in the mountains, or killed by roaming spiders? How will he protect himself if he's caught out in the wilderness at night? And if he manages to reach the distant village, how will young Ru deal with the surprise waiting for him there?

Book 2, Chapter 1

I looked up at the sun.

It felt like I'd been walking forever, but judging by the time, it was only late morning. In fact, when I turned around, I could still see the village far behind me.

Pitiful! Some journey so far. This would take forever!

Villagers never walked anywhere, I thought. My feet hurt, my back hurt. All the smithy work in the world hadn't prepared me for this.

"Never mind," I scolded myself. Suck it up and go...

I had to get to the big village *quickly* to figure out how to save my zombie parents. It would be terrible if they broke out of the basement while I was gone and ran away into the woods—or worse!

I walked faster. Got into a rhythm like I was hammering metal. Instead of 'Clang, Clang', I muttered 'stomp, stomp', and concentrated on moving forward...

Eventually, my little village was out of sight behind me, and only the road lay ahead...

Of the several gravel roads going to the big village where I was going, this one was the least traveled, and the trickiest. Since this road would go over the mountains, most travelers went to the big village by the easier roads that went out along the plains toward the coast and other villages. This mountain road, however, was the most direct route.

It sure was steep, though, so I'd heard.

These roads could take me anywhere, I realized. But the big village was where I needed to go. There was a huge library, and more importantly, the best librarian in existence. *Legendary*, they said. If anyone knew how to change my parents back from being zombies, the Legendary librarian *Bindr* would. And I would get that big village and its huge library, even if it killed me ... which it might.

Finally, I was making progress. Already, the terrain was beginning to change. I'd heard all kinds of stories about trees, giant waterfalls, strange creatures, and now I would get to see them in person.

I was excited! I'd always longed for adventure—to be a warrior—and this was my chance. I touched the hilt of the sword Brew gave me after I killed the spider that attacked him.

I could do this!

The path beneath my feet faded in and out with the patches of grass and earth.

I didn't really pay much attention—I just enjoyed the sunshine. My body was getting used to the exercise pretty quickly, so I just rocked along...

Suddenly, I saw a village!

Wow, was I already there? I thought. Had I been so *in the groove* that I'd crossed over the mountains without even noticing?

I picked up my pace to a trot. Pretty soon, as the buildings came into view, I saw a fence with a man sitting on it. Something seemed really strange. Familiar, almost. I ran up to the man, and it was our *own* librarian...

What?! What the blazes?

"Hi, Ru," he said. "I thought I might see you back here."

"Payj!" I exclaimed, flabbergasted. "How did you get here ahead of me?" I thought I had been hiking pretty quickly. Had my own village's librarian gotten ahead of me somehow; maybe with a shortcut? I was completely shocked, and more than a little upset. If Payj knew a secret, quicker route, shouldn't he have told me?!

The librarian shook his head, and his big nose bobbled. "Sorry to tell you, Ru," he said, "but you're not at the big village. You're back home."

I just stared at him, sure that my eyes were popping out of my head...

"What...?"

"There's a *reason* villagers never travel. Have you ever thought about it?" Payj continued. He patted the wood beside him, and I sat on the top of the fence next to him, resting my feet on the lower rail.

"Because ... we just enjoy our homes and family too much?" I offered, but I was pretty sure it wasn't the right answer.

The librarian made a 'tsk tsk' sound. "No, Ru. Not even close." He paused to look at the distant horizon. "It's our nature, as villagers. We are designed to stay close to home so that we tend to our crops and families. Thus, we villager people are part of the *cycle of life*."

"So?" I was not impressed.

"*So* ... strange things happen whenever we try to leave. Like, we circle around, and end up back at the village again." He leaned back smugly, almost losing his balance.

I felt my face turning red.

"Why didn't you tell me?" I demanded. "I've wasted so much time!"

Payj tipped off the rail, and leaned against it as if nothing happened. "*You* are so unusual and strong, Ru, and I wasn't sure that it would happen. If I told you, would you have believed me?"

"Absolutely not!" I replied fiercely, then I pondered. "So, what do I do?"

"I think once you get out of range, you'll be okay," he replied, stroking his chin. "We just need to get you there!" The librarian reached into his inventory and pulled out a piece of glass and handed it to me. "I've been thinking, Ru. I have a *theory*. If you take and use this piece of glass, you can head to the big village and always make sure that the sun is over your left shoulder. I mean, *make adjustments* if the road turns naturally. But if you try to keep the sun behind you, you shouldn't get turned around ... I think."

"Cool." I said catching on. "Good idea. That could work." I practiced holding the glass, and turned with it, watching the flare of the sun. "Yeah, love it! Is there anything else I should worry about? Anything *else* you want to tell me?"

Payj shook his head. "Maybe just that some people have gone off and never returned. We think that it's because they eventually *forget* about their village, and wander around until they find another. Then, they're attached to the new village..."

"I would never forget my home! Ridiculous!" But then again, I never expected to walk in a circle either. "Just in case, what can I do?"

The librarian handed me a little book. "If you forget what you're doing, Ru, open this. No—don't open it now. *Save it*, just in case." Payj clapped me on the shoulder. "Now good luck ... again! Be off with you! I'll check in on your parents on my way back to the library."

Bindr hopped down from the fence and strode off.

"Thank you Payj!" I yelled after him, then hopped down myself and turned, starting my journey *once again*. Blazes!

The second time, I paid more attention to where I was going.

The glass really did help, and I was able to make adjustments as I turned with the winding road up into the mountains.

There was one thing heavy on my mind, though. I was worried about forgetting my village. Exactly how far was the circling range that Payj had mentioned? Would there be a point where I'd forget, then another place where I'd remember again?

I stopped to eat a sandwich. There was a little tree a good ways off the main road, and it provided some shade, which was refreshing. As I ate, I saw a cloud of dust grow closer, coming down from the mountains. The cloud drew closer, aloud with a loud, plodding sound, then it passed me on the road. It was a knight with his small army. The horses were bucks, and they looked tired but happy. I wondered where they were all going.

Some of the soldiers waved as they rode by. One nice man stopped, approached me up the hill, and said, "What are you doing out here, villager?"

"Eating a sandwich," I replied.

"Do you need help of any sort?" he asked, hanging back.

"No, no thank you! Fare thee well!" I replied gaily. The warrior rode off, but looked back a couple of times. I didn't know why.

After a while, I finished my sandwich, and just sat enjoying the day. A little stream was babbling, and there were butterflies on the flowers.

A thought was tickling my brain: *Wasn't I supposed to be doing something?*

I was a little bored, so I decided to walk towards the mountains. They were a nice color.

Clang, Clang! With each step, I heard what sounded like metal hitting metal. Huh.

Well, whatever, I thought, then I kept my feet going to the beat...

A little song popped in my head:

I ... *clang*...

Hate ... *clang*...

Walking ... *clang*...

And ... *clang*...

I'd ... *clang*...

Rather ... *clang*...

Be out ... *clang*...

Fighting! ... *clang*...

And as long ... *clang*...

As I am bold ... *clang*...

I will continue ... *clang*...

Iron Smiting ... *clang*...

Nice! I noticed that I had a sword on my belt. *That* was cool. I stopped and took it off to look at the weapon. It had some etching, which was a little crooked...

The sword felt very important to me for some reason.

Was I a warrior?

But that man called me a villager.

I took a couple of swings with the blade, and I was amazing! BAM!

So ... a warrior indeed.

I walked some more, but the song and the crooked etching kept bugging me. It got so annoying that I decided to see if I had anything on me which might explain what I was doing or where I was going...

I emptied out my inventory, and there were some odd things in it: Horseshoes—though I had no horse—a map, and two books. I opened one of the books, and read that it was from someone named *Payj* directed to his friend, Bindr.

Am I supposed to deliver this? I wondered.

I opened the other book. It was filled with drawings, and started with, "Your name is Ru. You are a blacksmith and a warrior. You are on a journey to save your family and friends. Here is a drawing of your village." There was indeed a drawing. Then, the page followed up with, "You can do it, Ru! Your friend, Payj."

Oh, my Blazes!

The memories all came flooding back. *My mom! My dad!* My brother Brew and the zombie attack! How could I have forgotten?!

Without further ado, I threw up my sandwich.

Staring grimly down at the road, I started my journey *again*...

This time, I held the glass in one hand and the book of memories in the other. I was so freaked out that, every few yards, I would stop and read the book, then check my direction to make sure that the sun was on my back.

I seemed to be doing okay.

Holy Blazes—what if there were other problems that villagers had while traveling?! I'd better stay on my toes!

The mountain range was pretty close by now, and I was walking through little hills. There were pretty trees all around, and lots of rabbits, too. The sun started to get lower in the sky, and I realized that I had found another problem...

I smacked myself lightly on the head.

No shelter!

I forgot to take fire-starting things with me! What the blazes was I gonna do?! I couldn't stand in the middle of a forest in the dark and fight off zombies and wolves!

This was a disaster! But ... no matter—I had to keep going! My mom and dad were depending on me. Just the fact I even *remembered them* was a new victory.

"Look around, and use your head," I told myself. "What would *Dad* do?"

Up ahead, a small stream burbled, and my stomach grumbled in response.

Fuel the fire, I thought.

Blacksmiths always kept their fires fueled. *Right.* I'd better eat something, since my sandwich was left disgustingly by the side of the road.

I walked up to the stream and saw a nice, flat rock slightly off of the road. *Perfect!* I thought. I could get a quick meal, refill my water, then deal with the shelter problem.

Rummaging through my pack, I found a whole roast chicken and round of bread. Yum, my favorite! I ripped off a leg and began munching...

Oh, that was good! I thought, smiling.

I began on the other leg, then stopped when I heard a small sound. A big, grey dog was standing nearby, looking at the chicken leg in my hand. Sweet. I love dogs!

"Hello, fella!" I exclaimed. "Whatcha doing out here by yourself?"

The dog didn't wag its tail—it just stood there ... staring.

"Hey, good buddy. Where's your master?" I asked, then started to take another bite.

There was silence from the dog. It dawned on me, as the food was going into my mouth, that this may not be a dog. It might be a wolf.

As if reading my mind, the creature bared its teeth, and I screamed, and flung the chicken leg towards it! Pure reflex...

Instead of neatly catching the piece of roasted chicken as I expected, the canine let the chicken leg hit it right in the face. BAM!

Instantly, the dog's eyes turned red and it gave a low growl...

"It's a wolf," I muttered. "Not a dog— definitely a wolf..."

Moving as slowly as I possibly could, I packed my things, then stood.

The trees filled around me with red glowing eyes...

I had annoyed a wolf pack!

Letting out a huge holler, I flung the rest of my chicken and bread at the first wolf, then I ran for the hills as the pack descended upon my supper!

I desperately needed help—*desperately!*

Still running, I looked around, and in the dusky light, I saw a fire twinkling in the distance.

"Oh, good!" I cried, and hoofed it to the distant camp.

By the time I got there, running through the woods like a madman, it was pretty dark. The path wound through trees, and luckily, the fire led me to a small clearing right next to the road. That was good, because come morning, I wouldn't have to worry about getting lost!

There were four men were sitting around a little fire, laughing and eating. I hesitantly stepped closer. Hearing their horses nicker, I tiptoed over to the steeds to get a closer look.

All four horses were jet black, with unique, charred-gold armor...

They were the Blackened Knight's horses!

Oh, *blazes*...

Book 2, Chapter 2

Wow.

Now I had an awful choice: brave the dark? Or brave the soldiers?

I was tired, and there was no shelter anywhere. Maybe there was a cave somewhere nearby, but I couldn't see a thing, and who knows what nasty creatures would be inside if I found one? I longed to be inside somewhere and was tired of talking to myself.

Bad company would be better than *no* company, right?

Then I heard a howl in the darkness behind me, so quickly walked toward the fire and the men, happy with my decision. Before anyone detected my presence, I stepped into their circle of firelight.

"Uh, excuse me," I said.

Instantly, all four men jumped to their feet with their swords drawn!

"Wha...?!" one of them grunted.

"Hi there!" I exclaimed with a *big* smile on my face. I tried to look as innocent as I could...

"Who are *you?!*" one of them demanded, stepping toward me and pointing his sword at my face.

I put my hands up and let out a little laugh that probably sounded very nervous. "Oh, heh heh ... I'm nobody! I'm just a traveling villager looking for somewhere to stay the night. There are *wolves* out there..."

The soldiers looked me up and down. I kept a goofy smile on my face and pretended not to be afraid.

In truth, I was terrified...

One of the men snickered. How rude!

"I'll tell you what," said the biggest soldier. "If you do our dishes and get us more wood, we'll let you stay, villager."

"Sounds good to me!" I replied with a nod, as I heard the howls coming closer.

Hustling up to be among the four men, I quickly sat down on a log. Then, I scooted down the log because one soldier was *farting* noisily. It wasn't just the noise—it was the smell!

In fact, pretty soon I noticed that everyone else was staying away from Smelly too. (That's what I named him in my head—*Smelly*.)

I recognized one of the men. He was the one fighting with the three bullies back at the village at the Slithery's camp.

I knew it! I thought. These guys were no good, and they were mean, but I *needed* them. Blazes!

What was this guy doing with the rest of them? As I recall, they were beating him up pretty good, and it wasn't exactly in the spirit of training...

Well, I was not going to worry about it. It was not my business. The most important thing was that I had a safe place to spend the night.

The four soldiers gave me chicken too. It wasn't as good as my chicken— spiced and roasted carefully in the oven back home until it was *just right*—but it was food.

After dinner, the non-bully and I went out to gather wood. The man didn't say anything; he just pointed directions. He held a torch and sword—to guard me I supposed—and I picked up wood while he watched the dark woods.

Because of my strength, I was able to pick up a huge bundles. I started to carry a good bit of wood back to camp when my companion suddenly whispered, "Don't show them how strong you are." I put down half the bundle, then pretended to stagger under the weight.

When the other three soldiers saw me struggling, they were chuckled, then promptly stopped paying attention to what the other soldier and I were doing.

Jerks! I thought.

Gathering more wood, I managed to chat a little with the non-bully soldier. His name was Jack, and Jack seemed like a normal, friendly guy.

I was so tired! When the chores were done, I lied down on the ground as far away from the others as I could, with my back to a log, and fire warming me. Eventually, I got used to the smells and snores of the soldiers, and fell asleep...

Dreaming of my nice comfy bed and pillow, I woke in the middle of the night, startled by an unusual sound. My entire body hurt.

I kept thinking of my family, and hoped that my brother was okay, taking care of mom and dad, who were locked up in the basement.

Some of the soldiers snoring as loud as *cannon fire* eventually lulled me back to sleep...

The next morning, the soldiers were packing up.

"Where are you going?" I asked the men casually. Maybe I could stick with them. I had survived one night, after all.

"There's a hunting camp halfway up the mountain," Jack replied. "Sir Darwym likes rabbit, so we're going to capture a good supply, and take the meat back to our camp at your village. We'll be moving on to the coast after that." Jack stopped and stretched. Sleeping on the ground must be uncomfortable for him too.

"That's too bad," I said. "I'm headed to the big village."

Jack continued packing. "Well, if you go with us to the hunting grounds, there's a shortcut you can take from the camp. That'll cut a full day off of your trip!"

"Really?" I asked. "Interesting! Can you show me?"

I pulled out my map, and Jack pointed out the camp and the shortcut. It looked good, but I was learning that things weren't always as easy as they seem...

"I don't know," I replied, full of doubt. "What if I get lost?"

"I've been on the shortcut," Jack said confidently, "and it's not bad. But it's your choice..."

Wow. I imagined gaining a whole day. And I'd have company for at least one more night. Sweet!

I didn't ask. I just tagged along. Luckily, the terrain was getting steeper and the soldiers walked the horses, which made it easier for me to keep up.

The day wasn't bad. I gave the men plenty of space, and they ignored me, but I felt a lot safer being with four swordsmen.

The group of us went up and up, through the trees. The hills were getting extremely tall. We crossed a river, and by mid-afternoon, we had reached the hunting camp.

I could see why people hunted there. The shack was open—just a roof on poles with a back wall and a fireplace, but it was positioned to block the wind. A nice, solid fence provided protection, and a stream ran past, leading down to a meadow with *thousands* of rabbits!

Okay, maybe not thousands. But it was a *heck* of a lot...

"Rabbit Valley," Jack said.

"No kidding!" I replied. I'd never seen so many rabbits before!

The bullies went out hunting while Jack and I gathered a bunch of wood. Since the others couldn't see me, I carried huge bundles, and Jack and I were done in no time...

"Well, I guess I'll be going," I said, dusting off my hands.

"The shortcut is up that way," Jack said, pointing. "Good luck to you!"

I held out my hand. "Thanks for all your help, Jack."

The soldier smiled, and I felt like I'd made a friend.

I got about twenty yards toward where Jack had pointed when it started to rain.

It really poured!

With a shock, I realized that this was the *first time* I'd ever been outside in the rain, and I freaked out, running back to the shelter like a baby!

Jack was tending the fire, and looked up at me in surprise.

I immediately felt embarrassed.

"Villagers don't do rain," I said a little too quickly, and Jack laughed. I mean, seriously, we don't!

I noticed that Jack had a whole box of flints and iron nuggets. My fingers itched to take some. I really needed fire! But it wasn't right to steal, so I just ignored the stuff. Maybe I could ask for some later...

We took care of the horses, all of whom looked even more miserable because of the weather. The animals weren't getting rained on at least, but water was bouncing off of the ground and making their hooves wet.

"What's with this weird metal?" I asked, fingering the blackened gold metal on the saddles. In all my experience being a blacksmith, I'd never seen anything like it!

"Sir Darwym provides it," Jack said, "and uses it for most of our armor and weapons. I have no idea where it comes from, but it lasts longer than other metal, and it's very light! Here, check out my sword..." He handed his blade to me, and I looked at it curiously...

The strange metal looked like gold, which had somehow been scorched as it was forged. But it was so much stronger than gold—or even iron—and it had a weird *glow*. Jack's sword felt like it was vibrating in my hand!

I handed the weapon back to him. It didn't feel good to touch it...

"Yeah, and the armor vibrates too," Jack said. I must have given a disgusted look, because Jack suddenly became defensive. "Sir Darwym is one of the best knights around! It's an honor to train under him. I'm thankful for this weapon and armor!"

I didn't say anything about how miserable Jack looked. Perhaps the armor made him uncomfortable, just like the horses...

Eventually, the rain stopped. Apparently, rain didn't bother the bullies at all, because they came back loaded down with rabbit bodies.

Smelly tossed one at me and said, "Here, make yourself useful!"

I didn't know anything about skinning or butchering a rabbit. I mean—we always got our meat from the butcher, for blaze's sake, but Jack showed me how to prepare the meat.

One thing is for sure: fresh, hot rabbit stew is *amazing*.

I filled my belly, and stashed some for the morning. There was so much of it, the bullies didn't seem to mind me taking some. When the soldiers finished up munching on a roast rabbit, they threw the scraps and trash in a corner of the shelter. Apparently, they weren't worried about wolves. I envied them for their daring. Mom would have scolded me.

I was just about to lie down in a cleaner corner when I heard a soft sound near the scraps. Biggest (I started to call them all nicknames) heard it too, and before I knew it, the huge warrior had pounced onto something!

"Look here what I caught!" he grunted, holding something up by the scruff of its neck...

Loudest, who had fallen asleep on his back and was snoring, woke up with a series of snorts.

"What?!" He asked loudly—which is why I nicknamed him *Loudly*.

Biggest had caught a small, furry animal, which was doing its best to claw the man's eyes out.

It was not a rabbit.

It was an *ocelot!* The small beast was fierce, yellow and white, with black spots all over, stripes on its tail, and brilliant, green eyes!

Smelly stood and walked toward Biggest and the cat. I could swear the ocelot looked at Smelly and wrinkled its nose in disgust. "What a pretty, pretty kitty!" he said, poking it with a fat finger, which was a *big mistake*. With four paws free, the ocelot turned into a blazing ball of claws and fur!

"Yow!" Smelly shouted, jumping back. He looked at the cat angrily, sucking his dirty finger.

Biggest laughed. "Stupid!"

Smelly got a nasty look in his eyes, and said, "Put 'em down and hold him!"

Jack looked away, eyes closed. *Oh no!* Did that mean that Jack had seen something like this before? I got a bad feeling in my stomach...

Biggest laughed again, then bent down, putting the ocelot on the ground but keeping a strong hold on him...

Smelly got a stick of wood out of the fire, and said "I'll teach you to scratch me, cat! How do you like fire, eh?!"

Loudly started clapping in excitement. "Burn it! Burn it!"

Jack—his own terror matching the cat's—went over to Biggest and said, "Hey, let the little thing go!" But Biggest just scowled, then took one meaty hand and pushed Jack backwards so hard that the smaller soldier went flying!

"We're not gonna to kill it, you wuss," he told Jack with a sneer. "We're just have a little *fun* with it. Geez—whaddaya take us for?"

I was horrified.

The poor cat! It was just trying to get some scraps, after all! It was trash that nobody wanted!

Jack, a trained soldier, had stood up to the bullies and was easily overpowered. Biggest had barely lifted a finger. What could I do?! Nothing...

Smelly took the burning wood, and Biggest changed his grip to keep the cat pressed down against the floor. Holding the ocelot with one hand, he unwound its tail and held the tip of it out for Smelly...

Smelly lit the tail on fire.

The ocelot yowled, and I shouted, "No!" Biggest was so shocked when I cried out that he let go of the cat, who ran into a corner next to Jack. The nicer soldier quickly put out the fire by dunking its tail into a pail of water.

With a hiss, the flaming tail went out, and the cat let out a long, low growl...

All three bullies swiveled toward me. I could swear that their eyes turned red, like the wolves...

"Villager!" shouted Biggest, standing up to his full height. The man's head almost brushed the ceiling. "Villager, go get that cat and bring it over to me ... *now*."

He was going to do it again. He was going to make me let him...

My knees started shaking. I could barely stand.

Biggest took a step towards me, scowling, and Smelly stood to loom beside him. Somehow, Loudest had gotten around behind me. I was trapped...

What to do, what to do? My brain raced. I'd try ... *reasoning* with them!

"Oh, I'm sorry," I stammered with a broad smile. "I didn't mean to shout—I just didn't want you to hurt the cat, that's all..."

"And what business is it of *yours?!*" Loudly shouted.

"None—none at all! I'm sorry, guys! I'll just go *sit down over here*..." I took a step to get away toward Jack and the cat, and the three brutes stepped with me. "Or ... I'll go sit over *here*," I added with a nervous chuckle, taking a step in the opposite direction. Again, the three soldiers moved with me.

Smelly still held the burning stick, and said, "Since you spoiled our game, Villager, how about we burn *you* instead? Just a little?"

"It's only *fair*..." Loudly shouted, grabbing me from behind and holding my arms tightly.

I wiggled, but couldn't get free...

Biggest laughed again, and Smelly stepped forward, "First *you*, then the cat," he growled.

The three of them didn't know that I was a blacksmith; that I had worked with fire for my entire life. When the flaming stick touched my skin, the pain was just like it had been a thousand times before from sparks flying out of the forge.

But a wave of rage boiled up inside me...

This wasn't right. My mind repeated it over and over again: *This isn't right. This isn't right. This isn't right!* Before I knew it, I had flexed my blacksmith muscles, gotten free and punched each of them on the chin—one, two, three!

All three of the brutes toppled to the floor like cut-down trees, crashing into the dirt and cobblestone, their blackened-gold armor *clanging* as they collapsed.

Biggest, Loudest, and Smelly all lay in a circle around me, groaning.

Jack's jaw dropped. The ocelot stared at me with bright, green eyes.

Oh dear, I thought. Should I go back into peaceful villager mode? Or run for the hills?

They started to get up, one at a time, hands on their swords and evil in their eyes...

Okay, so peaceful villager was out, I thought with a grimace.

I could fight—I knew it. But somehow, my confidence broke, and I ran!

Brushing past Biggest, I knocked the huge jerk off of his feet, then ran to the corner. As quickly as I could, I grabbed my bag, the cat, and for good measure, a handful of flint and iron.

Then I was outta there!

When I heard the three evil soldiers' footsteps *thumping* through the dirt and gravel behind me, I didn't look back...

Book 2, Chapter 3

Filled with energy from the fight, I ran quickly up the path. For a while, I didn't know if they were *chasing me* or not, but I didn't slow down to take a look! The rain had stopped, but there were muddy puddles everywhere.

A small amount of fear trickled into me when I realized that the three brutes might get their horses, and then they could catch me for sure! I listened for horse hooves, peering into the dark forest as I ran, thinking of where I could dart off to from the path in case I needed to lose them in the tight trees...

The ocelot bounced in my arms, wound tight like a spring.

Luckily, the moon was peeping out from behind the clouds; a nice big moon. I could see where I was going without much trouble, which was great. I didn't want to run off of a cliff!

I slowed down after a while, then stopped to see if I was being followed. The path ran along a ridge, and I could see pretty well behind me.

Nothing. Good.

Whew, that was a close call. Those three mean soldiers could easily have pounded me after I made them so mad!

I stopped and rearranged my things. I wasn't sure what to do with the ocelot, so I put it in my shirt.

"Take it easy, kitty," I said. "I'm just going to carry you until I find somewhere dry and safe for you to stay." The creature seemed to understand me, because it just curled up and went to sleep against my chest. I could feel its wet tail against my skin, which reignited my outrage.

Someday I would make those jerks *pay!*

Since the moonlight was decent, and I seemed to be alone, I walked on for a while until I started to descend into a little valley filled with trees.

It was also getting late, the moon directly overhead. I had used up my energy spurt from my adrenaline, and was tired. *Exhausted*, really. Little circles of mist began gathering too.

I'd better find a place to sleep, I thought, looking around at the night.

But where...?

Maybe there was a little cave, or log, or something. I continued down into the valley, feeling uneasy and exposed. The cat moved around in my shirt and popped its head out, the rest of its body staying in a tight little ball. The creature was *purring*, which tickled, but made me feel better.

Hopefully the little animal wouldn't be scarred for life...

"Help me find a place for the night, Cat," I whispered. This creature had to know more about surviving in the wilderness then I did...

It did hear the wolf howls first.

The cat growled suddenly, and I looked around frantically...

"What is it?"

Then I heard the howls.

Just as quickly as they appeared, the howls seemed to grow closer. I saw a pair of red eyes emerge from the darkness. One of the wolves appeared sniffed at the air, and I wondered if it was the same wolf as before—the one who knew that I had roast chicken!

I looked around frantically for somewhere—anywhere—where I could get away...

There! I thought. A big tree with branches. I'd never climbed a tree before, but it seemed like now was the time.

Running toward the big tree, I saw a shadow dash past me. Then another. The quick-moving shades turned and I saw the red eyes congregating between me and the tree...

With all my strength, as I sprinted toward the tree, I jumped over the wolves in my way, aiming to catch a low branch. I felt a snap at my heel. I caught the branch, and propelled myself upward, climbing for my life!

"Please don't let wolves climb trees!" I stammered. "Please don't let wolves climb trees!" I climbed up and up until I could go no higher...

If wolves *could* climb, I'd be a goner...

But as it turned out, wolves can't climb trees. They don't need to—they can just wait until you fall out or have to go down, or until something more delicious comes along.

I was lucky. Over the course of the night, something ran by in the forest below, and the wolves all dashed off with a unified howl, chasing the creature away into the darkness.

Since I was in a huge tree, and safe from wolves at least, I decided that I wasn't going anywhere until daylight. I made myself comfortable as best I could, tying myself onto a branch so I wouldn't roll into any *waiting jaws* down below. I used my big pack as a pillow, and took the little cat out of my shirt. I was relieved that I hadn't squished it!

Hugging my sword, I fell asleep, or whatever you call it when you doze and wake up, listen, doze, and jerk awake again.

When I finally woke up for good the next morning, the ocelot was curled up in a ball by my head. The creature was nice and warm in the cool air, and I petted it.

"Nice kitty..."

It was dawn, and the birds were singing. It was a pretty day, and I was stuck up in a tree—way up. I hadn't realized how far off of the ground I was in the dark...

How would I even get down? I wondered.

Oh well—I had no choice.

I prepared my things and lowered them down, trying not to actually look in that dreadful direction. Every time I did look down, my head would swim...

"How do you get down a tree?" I asked the cat, who was sitting and watching me.

The spotted kitty turned and hugged the tree, using its sharp claws to go down, tail first.

It was a good an idea as any, so I tried the same, feeling for branches to stand on. After several cautious steps, I realized that it was like climbing down a crazy ladder.

Finally, I touched down into the grass.

Hooray! I thought. I was on the ground! It felt like a huge accomplishment, and I was pretty proud of myself!

But there wasn't much time to celebrate. My parents were zombies, and Brew and everyone else with zombified loved ones were waiting on me...

Time to go.

I wanted to leave the ocelot behind to continue its life, but the forest here didn't look like a very safe place. For one thing, I knew that it was full of wolves, and I didn't see any rabbits. If this little spotted creature would let me, I'd take it to a better spot. It would just take a little time...

If the cat was to travel with me, I'd have to give it a name. Without knowing how to tell the difference, I decided to consider the cat a 'she', and started running possible names through my head...

Seru, I thought. *Aimi. Kasumi. Wanda*...

The ocelot was smelling my backpack. The end of her tail was toasted and singed from the flames, and new name jumped out at me! It was just *temporary* of course—I'd find her a new home soon enough.

"Hey Smudge," I said with a smile. "Let's go find you a nice home!" Then, I held out my arms. I wasn't sure what I expected the cat to do, but she ran right up my body, and draped herself across my shoulders.

Cool, I thought, then, I remembered that I didn't *need* a cat. And now I had bigger problems. The most important thing was to save my parents and the other villagers. And for that, I needed to get to Bindr, the librarian. That big village couldn't be far now, right? I just had to—

"Uh oh," I said.

I had run off the path. How would I find it again?!

I swept the area with my eyes frantically...

Oh, I thought. *Right there*. Nice!

Smudge and I walked for maybe an hour until we came to a perfect spot for her for her to live her nice, ocelot life: a nice clearing with a stream, flowers, and lots of rabbits!

I was hungry, so I put Smudge down and pulled out some rabbit stew. I gave smudge some scraps of rabbit meat. We ate, enjoying the sunshine. Smudge drank a little water from the stream, and I knew that she'd be happy here...

Getting my things ready, I stood, watching little Smudge chase a butterfly. A big lump filled my throat...

Why in the world was I so sad??

"Goodbye, little cat!" I exclaimed, then swiftly turned and walked away.

I had checked the map during breakfast. According to it, once I was through this valley of Smudge's Meadow, I would climb another ridge, then start the descent down to the plains and eventually, the Big Village.

There was one more night to spend in the woods. I'd reach the village *tomorrow!*

I hiked all day.

By nightfall, I was nice and secure on top of the next ridge over. This time, I'd given myself plenty of time to find shelter and build a fire before the sun went down.

Before long, I'd located a great tree with a big log underneath. Putting my things up in the tree, I gathered a bunch of wood, then used the flint and steel I'd taken to start the flames.

With a log at my back, and a fire in the front, I'd be safe from animals—at least I hoped so. Of course, I'd sleep in the big tree just to be safe for sure. For dinner, I roasted a rabbit, and made sure to put all the scraps away.

The fire eventually died down, and I climbed up into the tree to lie down. I was just falling asleep when something furry touched my head!

Agggh! I jumped up and almost fell off of the branch!

What was that?! I wondered.

"Meow," something said.

It was Smudge!

I stared at the cat, and she stared at me. "You mean you followed me all day?!" I asked. I couldn't believe it!

For an answer, Smudge looked down at my pack, and touched it with a delicate paw. I instantly felt bad—she must be hungry. "Here," I said, sitting next to the ocelot. "Have some rabbit." Smudge ate most of the scraps, and she liked carrots, too!

After a quick wash with her front paws, Smudge curled up by my head. I was strangely pleased, but what in the heck was I going to do with a cat?!

I didn't realize when I fell asleep.

Smudge and I were sleeping soundly when a huge amount of noise woke me up.

Opening my eyes, groggy and confused, I heard someone shouting, "Help! Get away! Take that!" There were sounds of fighting ... and hissing!

It was a spider attack!

"Stay here," I ordered my cat. I grabbed my weapons and climbed down the tree, throwing wood on the coals so that I could find it again in the dark.

Once again, the moon was bright, and I ran quickly toward the chaos...

A man with his back against a rock was fighting three big spiders, while another arachnid crouched overhead, looking for a good chance to pounce...

I threw a horseshoe at the hidden monster, and again, my aim was perfect— BAM! Right in the forehead! The spider dropped like a stone at the man's feet, who kicked its body toward another spider.

"Ru, behind you!" Jack shouted. I recognized his voice—it was Jack! Turning, I had just in time to block a spider's pounce with my sword! I had never fought a real monster with my sword before. I'd killed zombies, sure, that night when the village was attacked. But they were slow, and had no skill.

Spiders were completely different. Not only were they super speedy, but they had eight legs, fangs, and poison!

"Aggggeeeeee" I shouted in a terrified war cry! The spider lunged at me, and I cut a leg off, then it scratched me with another. The arachnid reared to deliver a death blow, but I was faster, and I thrust in through its throat, sinking my blade up to the hilt!

The monster kept moving, thrashing frantically around...

"Where the heck is a spider's *heart?!*" I yelled.

"Just keep stabbing it!" Jack yelled back.

So I did.

I kept hacking at the thing. It was the same color as the forest behind it, and at times I could barely tell where the arachnid was, save for its glowing eyes. Eventually, the nasty creature stopped moving, so I turned to help Jack.

From a distance. With a horseshoe.

We killed a second big spider.

Now, there was only one left! This spider was the smallest and fastest. The hissing creature was fighting too close to Jack to let me to throw a horseshoe, so I charged in with my sword!

Jack kept four legs busy and I kept the other four legs busy. Eventually, we drove the thing off, and it scuttled away into the night, its legs rattling through the leaves!

We both stood, breathing hard, watching the darkness where the spider had run off to for a while...

I picked up everything the spiders had dropped: eyes and string. You never knew when such things could come in handy!

When I made my way back to Jack, I saw that the soldier was wounded. What in the blazes was he doing here?! I helped Jack over to the fire, and sat him down, taking his armor off. A spider's fangs had pierced his arm, and his skin was turning a nasty color...

Jack merely pulled out bottle from his pack, and splashed some of the liquid inside on his wound. Right away, the puncture marks started to heal!

"Neat!" I exclaimed. "Is that a *potion of healing?*" I'd heard about them, but never seen one before.

Jack looked up at me tiredly. "Hey Ru. Thanks for your help back there. Yeah, we all get a couple of healing potions to carry with us—standard issue."

"Nice. What are you doing out here? Are you hungry?" Fighting those spiders sure made *me* hungry. "I am." Without waiting for an answer, I climbed up the tree again. Smudge was snoozing, making soft little kitty snores. She was so cute...

I grabbed some things, then dropped back down.

Jack stared at me.

"So now you climb trees?" he asked. "And you kill spiders with horseshoes? What kind of a villager are you?!"

Embarrassed, I shrugged. "I just do what I have to do. What are *you* doing here?"

Now it was Jack's turn to look embarrassed. "Back there," he said, sheepishly, "when you fought to save the cat, it really showed me how much I've changed. I used to be like you. But after years of being around *them*, and being bullied by them, I became ... different. I couldn't stand it anymore! I'm no longer with Sir Darwym."

I looked at his armor. "You kept your gear..."

"I've earned it, Jack replied grimly. "Besides," he continued with a grin, "there's no way I'm going out into the wilderness barehanded, like you! You're nuts!"

The soldier tossed a piece of wood onto the flames. "Let's keep this fire going, okay?"

"Good idea," I replied. I'd had enough of spiders and wolves.

The moon was low in the sky, so we waited out the rest of the night sitting around the fire. When morning came and the world lightened again, I saw that Jack was checking his wound. I looked at it too— his arm was completely healed!

We chatted about our travels for a while until the topic of Jack coming after me came up again.

"I also wanted to make sure you were okay, Ru. I was worried, because you came running back before when it rained. I guess I should have known that you'd be alright..."

"Barely!" I exclaimed with a scoff. Who knows what calamity would be next?

"What ever happened to the ocelot?" Jack asked. "I don't think they would have hurt it, you know," he said doubtfully, "but that was the *final straw* for me!"

As if to answer, Smudge suddenly appeared, clawing her way down the tree, then leaping lightly from branch to branch. She paused, stretching long and yawning wide.

"There she is!" I exclaimed.

"*She?*"

The ocelot landed on the ground and approached Jack.

"Smudge, Jack. Jack, Smudge," I said, performing introductions.

Smudge rubbed up against Jack's leg, purring.

"All is forgiven I see," Jack said with a weary smile. "Thank you Smudge." The soldier scratched behind her ears. "I *am* sorry, little one..."

"Meow," she said.

And that was that.

"We're almost there, by the way," Jack said, pointing to a distant hill—now revealed by the morning light—while stopping to rub his foot. He put his boot back on. "Oh, dang—why didn't I take some *horses?*"

Horses would have been nice, even though I didn't know how to ride. But how hard could it be? *Something for the future*, I thought, after I find the Bindr the librarian, and figure out how to save my parents...

After gathering our things, we continued the journey to the big village.

We crested the last hill that Jack had pointed out earlier while Smudge ran along ahead. My heart was beating fast. After half a day of walking, our goal was finally in reach. It looked like we'd reach the village at lunchtime!

I stepped around the last rocks and looked down into a huge valley. Before us, in a patch of sunshine, was the Big Village.

We had done it!

Book 2, Chapter 4

It took us the rest of the day to get down to the Village, and by then—the sun low and colorful on the horizon—the library was *closed*. A small sign on the door said:

See you in the morning. Don't bother me.

-Bindr, the Librarian.

I went to knock anyway, and underneath the knocker was a tiny sign that read, '*And I mean it!*'

"Do we just ignore it?" Jack asked. "This is important, right?"

I shook my head. "I need this *Bindr* to be helpful. We'd better wait until the morning." I hated to say it, but there didn't seem to be an alternative.

"Meowrt," said Smudge. She was riding in her favorite place: under my shirt. I scrunched my chin down to look at her.

"Hungry, Smudge?"

When we were heading into the village, I was so focused on getting to the library that I had barely noticed my surroundings. The village was huge, and with plenty of time on our hands, I looked around...

The Big Village was about six times the size of my village. Not only was it big, but it was loud. The streets were filled with people of all shapes and sizes, most of them talking fast and trading with each other.

Some of the villagers were hard to understand, but I felt an odd stirring of excitement building inside me.

Ooh, a blacksmith shop! I thought, seeing the obvious sign down the street. I had to see what it was like! Jack and I walked over to check the place out, and saw two blacksmiths hard at work, obviously a father and son.

Before I knew it, tears welled up in my eyes. I opened my mouth to speak to the smiths—I just missed my family so much! But I didn't have anything to say, so I turned away. All the adventure and excitement drained out of me...

"Come on, Ru," Jack said. "Let's find a hot meal and a place to stay."

"Okay," I responded gloomily.

It was easier said than done. The BV (Big Village) was full of fighters gathering for a tournament. Most of the homes had signs on their doors saying, 'No Beds,' and I was starting to get discouraged. The sun was getting low. Would zombies come out and attack a big village like this when the sky turned dark like back home?

"I think I know a place," Jack said. "I stayed there before, back when I was with Sir Darwym's men."

"Well, let's try it," I replied. "You still have the armor on. You could wear it for years, and no one would know that you left, huh?"

Jack scoffed. "We'll see..."

We walked down a couple of streets to the biggest inn on the block. The place was loud, and bright, and packed with people wearing very nice things.

Pushing past all those nicely dressed people, all clean and neat, made me realize I had been traveling and fighting and probably coming off more like the rank soldier, Smelly, than someone like them, so I turned to leave...

"Let's try it," Jack said, and tapped the owner on the shoulder.

"Sorry, no room," the man answered without looking, then he turned around. When the innkeeper saw Jack's armor, he immediately changed his tune. "Oh—I'm sorry, sir! We do have one room available, if that would be all right?"

"Oh course," Jack said with an awkward smile. "With two beds, and we have a cat."

The man's eyes bulged a little bit, but he led us upstairs. "Great," he muttered, likely assuming that I couldn't hear him. "A cat—so much for the new mattress..."

When the innkeeper closed the door behind him and was gone, we fell onto the bed laughing.

"Did you see his face?" I asked, then imitated Jack's voice, "...and we have a cat!"

"Haw, haw," Jack laughed. Then he stopped and said, "But did you see his eyes? He was *afraid* to say no to me when he saw the armor..."

"Yeah, that's bad." I didn't like it one bit, come to think of it. Then I yawned.

"Well there's nothing we can do now but eat and get a good night's sleep. Who knows what will happen tomorrow...?"

Smudge roamed around the room. I gave her some rabbit, which I was sick of, and milk.

It was *heaven* to spend the night in a real bed. There were fluffy pillows smelling sweetly of chicken feathers and sunshine. I never thought in a million years that I'd be missing my boring, normal, comfortable bed and pillow back home...

"Go to sleep" I told myself. "Tomorrow will be here too soon..."

Morning brought fresh bread and coffee. Oh Blazes, I missed such mundane things!

Jack and I carried our things downstairs instead of leaving them in the room, and Smudge rode on me. I wasn't sure that I wanted to stay at the inn again, not where people were afraid of us and all...

If we were still here tonight, it might be better to sleep in a tree or on the ground.

We made our way back to the library, but a block, two hard men stepped out in front of Jack!

"What's going on?" I blurted, feeling my hand fall on the hilt of my sword. Smudge scrambled to get into my shirt.

One of the men carried a hammer. "You won't be staying long, will you?" he asked, menacingly.

Jack hesitated for a second, but then his training as a soldier kicked in. He stepped forward, hand on his own sword hilt, and spoke up. "Are you speaking to a *soldier of Sir Darwym* with such a tone?"

The second man wavered, maybe suddenly having second thoughts, then stepped backwards. The first man with the hammer, however, stepped up to the challenge.

Great—another bully! I thought, moving behind Jack, reaching for a horseshoe in my pocket.

The second man suddenly turned and ran away, and the first, seeing there were two of us and one of him, merely said, "Enjoy your visit!" and left as quickly as he could without actually running.

After a minute of letting the dust settle, Jack and I shared glances.

"I think I'd better do something to hide this armor," Jack remarked quietly.

"I'll make you some new armor when this is all over," I replied. "Armor that suits you." It was a promise, and I meant it.

After walking another block, I smiled when I saw the huge building appear where I was expecting it to be, our destination.

"Ah, there it is, finally!" I exclaimed with a grin. *The library!*

Success!

The door was open, and we could hear someone singing inside.

A village cat sat in the window, and Smudge jumped out of my shirt to visit it. Soon, there were two fur-balls snoozing in the sun of the windowsill.

The two story building was packed head-to-toe with book shelves that were likewise packed with books. There must have been *thousands* of them! A big staircase led to a second floor, and sunshine streamed in from the skylights.

"Hello?" I called, eager to find out how to save my parents. I bet I sounded like I was smiling. At last, I made it, and soon, Mom and Dad would be back to normal!

The Librarian came out, carrying a stack of books.

"Hello, how can I help you today?" the young man asked cheerfully.

Was that the right guy? I figured that Bindr would be older—this librarian seemed to be younger than Payj, the librarian from my own village.

"I bring greetings from Payj the Librarian of my home village. We need your help." I said, rather formally.

The librarian looked confused.

"Payj?" he asked, putting the stack of books down, then scratching his head.

"Your friend Payj," I replied. "You're *pen pals*, aren't you? Here—he sent this book for you..."

The librarian took the book, cracked it open, then read the first page.

"Ah," he said with a flat smile. "You don't want *me*, you want my uncle, Bindr!"

Okay, I thought, feeling panic rise up inside me. *Just a little hiccup. Let's find Bindr.*

I remained pleasant. "Sure. Can we talk to him?"

The nephew shook his head. "I'm sorry, friend of page. My uncle Binder is not here. Is there some way that I can help you myself?"

Gritting my teeth, I took a few minutes to explain about how my parents

227

were now zombies, and our village librarian was sure that Bindr would know how to cure them. Jack watched with sympathy growing in his eyes.

"Oh yes," the young librarian replied, nodding his head. "I'm sure that he'd know where to find that information!"

We were so close! I wanted to scream in frustration, but instead, talked very, very slowly. "When will your uncle be back?"

The nephew shook his head again. "I'm so sorry to say, tsk tsk. He will *never* be back. I am the librarian now."

Seeing that I was about to explode, Jack stepped in. "Well perhaps you could tell us where to find him?" the soldier asked.

"Afraid not," the librarian replied, furrowing his brow.

For a librarian, this man knew *nothing* about giving out information! Ridiculous!

Again, Jack stepped in. "Can you please tell us what happened to him, where he might be—anything that could help us?"

"You don't know what happened to him?" the librarian said suddenly. "Interesting..."

"If you don't *tell us already*, I'm gonna rearrange your books!" I said through gritted teeth, which was the biggest threat I could come up with to a librarian.

He raised one eyebrow, as if he dared me to, but finally delivered after some thought. "My uncle, the man you're looking for, was struck by lightning last week. He is now a *witch*, and is no longer a librarian."

A giant scream resounded though the library. People stuck their heads out from behind books, and one old lady said, "*Shh!*"

"Sorry!" I said. "I didn't mean to scream."

"It's alright," the librarian replied. "I understand that you're under stress! Please don't do it again," he said sternly.

I nodded, red-faced. The old lady who shushed me muttered something involving the word 'barbarian'.

Bindr's nephew continued: "Although my uncle is now a witch, it's possible that he might remember a few things. If you ... ah ... want to risk upsetting a witch!"

"I thought you said that you don't know where he is...?" Jack said, keeping his voice to a whisper.

"I *don't* know where he is, but I know where he might be." A scream threatened of excitement to escape again. I managed to control it this time, but the librarian must have seen it bubbling, for he continued without prompting. "He might be building himself a witch hut..."

"And where might he be doing that?" Jack asked, taking over for me since the stress of it all was making me giddy. I needed to find Bindr to save my parents—it was so important! And now, he was a witch?!

The librarian gave us directions— actual directions! "But it's a long shot," he added in the end. "Usually people forget everything when they turn into a witch. I said *hello* to Uncle Bindr the other day, and he didn't remember me at all!"

Jack and I exchanged glances. Didn't remember his own nephew? Hmm...

"Well I don't see any other options," I said. "Search through every book? Ask every stranger if they know how to cure being a zombie? Try the next village?"

Both Jack and the librarian shook their heads. Even the old lady popped her head over her book and joined in expressing her doubt.

Great, I thought. All my hopes to save Mom and Dad were resting on an evil witch. Curse that lightning bolt!

Book 2, Chapter 5

Before Jack and I left the library, Bindr's nephew asked me, "How did you get past the *triple villager's curse?*"

I didn't know what he was talking about, so I just shrugged.

"Come on Smudge," I said, turning to go. The cute, young ocelot ran over and jumped up onto my shoulder, and I strode back outside, out of that torture hole. What a weird place; everyone was so touchy and rude, and I was a blacksmith—I was used to making noise. Trying to be quiet all the time was silly.

"Wait," Jack said, hustling after me. "What three curses? What's he talking about?"

"I don't know," I replied, not caring. That librarian was a weird one, and unless he had more to say about finding Bindr, I didn't really want to hear about it. "Let's just get to the witch..."

"Stay here," Jack commanded, then ran back into the library.

I sighed, then sat on the library steps, looking around. BV was a beautiful village, busy and full of life. It would sure be interesting to be a blacksmith in such a large place with so many customers. Nice people, too. Some villagers smiled at me as they passed. I remembered the old lady in the library shushing me and chuckled. As silly as it was, something felt nice about how she cared so much about the town library...

Smudge hopped off and chewed on a blade of grass. She could be happy here, too—she had already made a friend. Looking back at the library windows, I could see the other cat sitting in it, watching us.

Across the street and a few blocks down, I could see the blacksmith's shop. Maybe they could use an extra hand? They looked nice...

Jack came hurrying back out of the library.

"Ru!" he exclaimed, face full of worry, pulling me to my feet. "We need to go—now! Come on, Smudge!" he said, grabbing the cat, who did not appreciate it. She scratched at him, and he put her in a bag. Angry meowing could be heard from inside.

"What's the hurry?" I asked. "Let's go check out the blacksmith's shop again. I feel like talking to them now..."

"We need to get out of this town *now!*" Jack insisted.

"Nah."

I kind of wanted to stay. I liked this place...

Jack said, "Well, sorry my friend. You're under the *triple curse*. If you don't leave now, you'll want to stay in this village forever!"

"That actually sounds kind of nice," I said. "I *like* this village."

When I looked up at Jack, grinning, he suddenly punched me in the jaw!

Everything went black...

I have no idea how Jack got me out of town.

Later in the day, I came to in a field, with Smudge sitting on my chest. The ocelot was purring, staring intently into my eyes. My jaw hurt.

"What the Blazes did you *hit me* for, Jack?!" I asked, dumping Smudge into the grass as I sat up angrily.

The soldier was leaning against a stump, chewing on a dandelion. He casually threw a leaf at Smudge, and she pounced at it. Apparently she had forgiven him.

"The triple curse," he said, as if that explained everything.

"You're just like that librarian! Don't give me that cryptic mumbo jumbo—tell me what you mean!"

"Sorry," he replied. "I guess it must have rubbed off. Okay. There's this thing called *the triple curse* that affects villagers. It's not really a *curse*, but three things happen if villagers—like *you*, Ru—leave their village."

"Oh yeah," I muttered, remembering the problems I had leaving him. "I circled back to my village at first, then, I totally forgot about it, later, before I ran into you! But what's the third curse?"

"If a villager—you—goes into another village, you'll want to stay there forever." Jack said it simply, without judging me.

I cried. Literally, big old sad tears.

This was just *too much*—I had almost failed Mom and Dad and Brew and stayed in the BV forever!

Jack stood by with sympathetic eyes, and waited as I just let it all out...

After a while, this flood and ocean of emotions building up—the guilt, pressing need, desperation, fear, the difficulties—died down, as if I was emptying a bucket in my chest, and I was done.

"Thank you," I said at last. "I really owe you one, Jack."

"Hey—we're helping each other! That's what friends do," he said, helping me up. "Come on now, let's find that witch Bindr, and save your parents, and then you can make me my armor! Deal?"

The new librarian had given us good directions after all, and luckily, Bindr's nephew thought that his uncle might be building on a piece of property only a little ways up the hill outside of town. That was good, because apparently, witches tend to make their territory miles away in a swamp.

The property where Bindr was likely to be was still in the village area—just outside of town—but I wasn't having any problems wanting to stay in BV anymore. Maybe the closer you were to the center of town, the more powerful the curse would be...? I had no idea...

Jack and I trudged up the hill, eventually coming to a clearing in the woods. In the middle of the stretch of grass was a little wooden house on stilts. Even though the clearing was sunny and green, there was something dark and gloomy about it—something in the air that made me a little uncomfortable...

"I've seen witch huts before," Jack whispered, "but this is really different. They usually don't have stairs, for one thing. And there are no pumpkins here..."

"What?" I asked. "Do witches like pumpkins or something?

"I don't like pumpkins," a cranky voice exclaimed from somewhere, "and I like stairs! How else am I supposed to go in and out?"

Jack and I both jumped and gasped.

Out of the hut popped a gangly man in dark robes and a big, black hat. He was a witch, and he came running down the stairs at full speed, flinging liquid at us! There was the sudden shattering of glass, and I got it full in the face. I immediately realized the witch had thrown a potion!

I'm poisoned! I thought with a flush of panic.

Actually, as it turns out, it wasn't poison. But it might as well have been. Jack was splashed too, and the soldier turned to me, trying to pull his sword in *slow motion*, and said something. His voice sounded terribly low, like an iron golem's voice, and I didn't understand.

"Whhaaaatttttt?" I asked, surprised at the lowness of my own voice.

"Weeeee'vee beennnn splasss—"

"Oh for goodness sake!" exclaimed the witch, glaring at us. "I splashed you two with a *potion of slowness!* Put that sword away, you, and both of you come into the hut. By the time you make it up the stairs, it will have worn off..."

I nodded, and the witch didn't even wait for a full nod; he just threw up his hands and walked away.

Smudge, who had not been splashed for some mysterious reason, followed him.

"Meow!"

"What a nice ocelot," the witch said, "Would you like some milk?" Smudge meowed again before I had even taken another step.

This was going to be a long day...

Jack and I *slowly* made our way to the hut. Climbing the stairs took forever, but by the time we reached the top, we were moving faster. Talking while slow was useless, so I just thought about all of the things I wanted to ask.

I thought about my parents, and my journey so far. It had been quite an adventure.

We finally got to the door.

"Come on in!" said Bindr, the witch. "Welcome to my home. Have some milk and cookies. I can sense that you mean me no harm, so I will allow this visit. But change your minds, and I will *destroy you!*"

Jack and I sat down with nervous glances at each other, almost at normal speed again.

We ate cookies. *Blazes*, they were good! Freshly baked!

"I'm Bindr," the witch said. "Who the blazes are you?!"

Taking a sip of milk to clear the crumbs out of my mouth, I coughed, wiped my mouth with my sleeve, then said, "My name is Ru. I'm here because—"

"Not now!" Bindr snapped. He looked at Jack. "Who are you?!"

"Jack."

"Hmph. Ru. Jack. Now that I'm no longer a librarian, I have time to do all sorts of things." Bindr said. "Like *baking*. It was *torture*, tending to all those books full of information that I could never use. The cookbook section alone back the in the village library has ten shelves of books! Do you know how many books there are on cooking with pumpkins?!"

"Um..." I said. "I don't...?"

"Twenty-two!" Bindr replied shrilly. "There are twenty-two books on cooking

Diary of a Warrior Villager
Book 1-4 - Ru's Adventure Begins!

with pumpkins, and I can remember than all—and I don't even like pumpkins! So many books, and no time to do anything with them!"

That reminded me.

"Bindr," I said, earning a scowl. "I've got a book for you here from Payj," I said. "May I have another cookie, please?"

"Payj!" Bindr exclaimed. "My old friend! Of course you can have another cookie, Rule," Binder said, handing me the whole plate.

"That's *Ru*." I scarfed the plate down. Cookies were awesome!

Bindr snatched the book then skimmed through it, laughing and chuckling. When he got to the part about the zombie attack and my parents, he looked at me with sadness in his dark eyes.

"I'm *so sorry*, Ru. What a terrible thing! And you've traveled so far. And you've gotten past the *triple curse!* Amazing!"

"Thank you," I replied. "Do you know of a cure?"

"Yes, yes I believe I know just the book!"

My heart leapt with joy. *At last!*

We spent that night in Bindr's hut. I had a hard time sleeping because of the excitement, and my jaw hurt from Jack's sucker-punch. Of course, by the time the slowness potion wore off, it was late—too late to get back to the village. Besides, I didn't want to stay *there* another night, not with that dreadful *triple curse*. What if I needed another punch on the jaw?

The next morning, my jaw was mighty sore, and I asked Jack if he had any of his healing potion left. When Bindr overheard us, he rushed over, shoving glass vials at us excitedly.

"Oh, I have loads of those!" Bindr exclaimed. "Why didn't you speak up? I'd be more than happy to see my potions tested on—I mean *given to* you both..."

After holding my nose and swallowing a stinky, red potion, I felt a strange warmth pass through my entire body, and my jaw felt fine—totally back to normal.

Lesson learned!

After some coffee and freshly baked bread, it didn't take Jack, Bindr, and me long to get to the library back in BV...

When we exclaimed, the young librarian who'd given us directions was truly shocked to see the transformed man.

"Uncle!" he exclaimed. "Do you remember me?"

"Um ... would you be *my nephew?*" Bindr asked, winking at us.

I made a mental note to ask Bindr how he remembered everything from his life as a villager. Apparently, new witches forgot entirely about their old lives, but Bindr seemed fine. Maybe a little crazy and manic, but fine. The witch walked right up the stairs to the left corner, third shelf from the left. From that shelf, Bindr plucked out a little book bound in leather.

"Here we are," Bindr said, returning to the ground floor and taking the book to a big table. "Let's see ... zombie, zombie,

zombie skeleton, zombie pigman—*ah!* Here it is!"

I took a deep breath. "Tell me..."

"Good news, Ru! It *can* be reversed! We just need ... a *potion of weakness* and a golden apple, both items for every person afflicted."

"Yahoo!" I exclaimed, grabbing the old lady and swinging her around in a circle. This time, the cranky old bat didn't shush me. "Where do we get them?"

"Witches make potions," Bindr said with a sly grin. "And we can make golden apples if we need to. They're really expensive, whether we buy them or make them, but it can be done."

Jack and I shared glances, then looked back at Bindr. He looked back at me with a twinkle in his eyes...

"So...?" I asked.

"So what?!" Bindr replied.

"I guess we need a witch. Will you help us?"

"Of course, boy!" he replied. "In fact, now that I'm free from this library, I'm going to travel with you to your village, and visit my old friend Payj."

"Whoo!" That's great news!"

"Be warned, however," Bindr said with a stern look. "You *are* still cursed. I'm just a *novice* witch, and the *potion of slowness* was my first creation. You can see, if you were paying attention, that it was way too strong. I'll have to practice! We wouldn't want to hit your zombie parents with a too-strong *potion of weakness* and have them *melt* or something, would we?"

I shook my head, unable to voice my disapproval.

"You can do that?" Jack asked.

Bindr ignored the question and went on. "We need to get the ingredients which we might not be able to buy. Golden apples are terribly expensive, and we need money one way or another for them..."

"But you're *in*, right?" I asked anxiously. I needed him! With the help of a witch, who used to be a legendary librarian, we couldn't go wrong, right? My parents would live again...

As if he hadn't heard me, Bindr continued: "Plus, I don't know if I'm cursed or not, since I'm a villager turned witch. I have my knowledge and charming personality now, but what if I start to turn *full* witch?"

"Jack will be with us," I replied, staring at Jack. "Right, Jack?"

The soldier looked a little surprised—perhaps imagining Binder turning on us—then nodded. "Absolutely, Ru. And Smudge too. But don't forget I'm on the run from Sir Darwym. If I get caught, they'll probably *kill me*. You too, Ru, after you knocked out three of his men. You're a target now..."

The situation overall was more than a little daunting. The three of us sat in silence for a moment, then the old lady said, "Well when do we leave?"

We roared with laughter.

Sure, there were obstacles. But we had to save the village and my parents!

Together, I thought, *we just might*

pull it off...

Book 3

The Apple Prize and Spider Eyes!

Ru, Jack, and the ocelot Smudge finally made it to the Big Village, only to find that the legendary librarian they were seeking is now a witch! And when Bindr the witch joins their cause, revealing what Ru has to do to save his parents, will a novice witch give them the edge they need to gather the ingredients required to turn Ru's mom and dad and everyone else back to normal?

And when some unforeseen horsing around ruins some of their progress, how will Ru the warrior villager free his parents from the zombie curse with so much going wrong?!

Book 3, Chapter 1

Sunshine streamed through the high windows of the massive library of *Big Village*. Scores and scores of book spines faced me from all directions and multiple floors of shelves—books of all sorts of colors. This place was *way* bigger than the little library back home!

The old lady sitting near me replied to the conversation I was having with Jack and Bindr.

"Well, when do we leave?" she asked.

We roared with laughter.

I looked around at the group sitting at the library table with me. If anyone could help me turn my parents back to normal from their *zombieness*, it would be these guys...

I was happier than I'd been in a long time, since before the zombie attack, and before my parents freaked out because I wanted to be a warrior. Here I was— actually on an epic journey—fighting monsters and breaking curses. *Nice!*

"What's the first thing we should do?" asked Jack.

"Let's get a bunch of reference books and take them back to my witch hut," Bindr the novice witch replied. "We can make my hut our *secret base!*" Bindr stood and began rummaging around the shelves, humming happily and pulling out book after book.

The Librarian—Bindr's nephew—looked aghast. "Uncle, you can't take *all* of those books! Those are in the *special reference section*. Not a *one* of those books is allowed to leave this building!"

"Don't be silly, nephew! I may have been zapped into a witch but I am *still* the head librarian!"

Binder did not pay any attention more to the boy, and instead began organizing books into stacks on our table. The young librarian turned away, and I wondered whether or not he was happy that his uncle was still the big boss. *Probably not*, I thought.

I tried to make the nephew feel better. "Hey look—you took over, and you're running things pretty smoothly, I see! I'm sure your uncle and the *whole village* is happy to have you be the new Librarian. Isn't that right, Bindr?"

Bindr ignored me, and I kicked him as he walked by.

"What?! Oh ... *right*, Nephew! You're doing a fine job. Thanks for stepping in..."

"Aaaand..." I continued, putting a hand on the nephew's shoulder, leading him away, "Bindr is going to be *very busy*

268

helping us. In fact, he's got a whole new career, now that he's a witch!"

The Librarian looked a little happier, especially when the little old lady patted him on the shoulder and added, "You're doing fine, dear."

Jack suddenly stood and said, "Wait a minute! I think we'd better talk about what we're gonna do. We need a plan of action!"

It was a good idea. I had a couple of things I was wondering about myself.

"Keep talking Jack," I said, turning back to my group.

Jack started pacing around the table, waving his hands as he talked.

"Alright, in general, we need to make the *potion of weakness*, and collect golden apples, right?"

"Wait, wait," said Bindr, grabbing a book and quill. "Ready. Go."

Jack resumed walking and talking. "Once we have those things, we need to get back to Ru's village. *Then*, we turn everyone back into villagers, starting with Ru's parents. *That's* the big campaign..."

Right so far, I thought. There was only one thing bothering me. I spoke up. "I'm worried about my parents. Can we go back home now? How about we do all of the brewing and collecting stuff there— back in my village?"

Bindr shook his head. "I think we have more resources here. And I'm sorry to say it—because I know you're worried—but we're just not sure what's been happening down there while you've been gone."

Smudge jumped up onto the table and sat on a pile of books. "Meowr," she said, comfortingly.

I put my head in my hands. "Arg. You're right, Bindr. I just want to *get back!*"

"We'll get there," Jack said, with a mix of steel and sympathy in his voice. I was lucky to have such great companions.

The soldier continued. "Now ... the smaller parts are: brew the potion of weakness. And that requires, Bindr...?"

The witch consulted another book. "A *brewing stand*," he said. "I have one already. Blaze power. I have a *little*, but not enough. Water bottles ... easy." He spoke and scribbled notes at the same time. "Spider eyes ... and mushrooms. The grocer should have mushrooms. Sugar ... we have tons here."

"Where do we get spider eyes and blaze powder?" I asked. I didn't even know what blaze power was! But spider eyes—I knew way too much about that. "How many eyes do we need? Is there a witch shop around here?"

Bindr stared at me as though a hammer hit him square in the head. "*Witch shop!*" he exclaimed with a touch of mad glee. "What a *great idea!*" I could see the wheels turning behind his wide eyes and spreading grin. Bindr turned to his nephew and shouted across the library, "Nephew! You are now *officially* the head librarian! I'm going to open a shop as soon as I get back!"

His nephew beamed with happiness, going so far as to quietly say, "Whoo Hoo!" Then he shushed himself and got back to work.

I was very happy for both of them. "Okay ... but ... is there a shop *now?*"

Bindr shook his head and chucked with delight. "No! Of course not! That's what makes it so great! I can open a shop— one that carries supplies and potions. There's no competition! Once it's profitable—which will be right away—I could open up a new shop in *every village!*"

"So ... where do we get blaze powder?" Jack asked. "And does anyone have extra spider eyes laying around?"

"Let me see..." Bindr muttered, his eyes darting around as he pondered. "I ordered a brewing stand starter kit, and it came with just a *tiny bit* of blaze powder.

But it would take too long to order more."
The witch muttered more under his breath,
flipping through the books. "Another reason
why my shops will be a hit! Now... blaze ...
blaze powder..." He cleared his throat and
read: "Blaze powder can be made from a
blaze rod. This rod is dropped by a *blaze*
once it is killed. From the rod, you can craft
blaze powder." He clapped the book shut
with a poof of dust. "Obviously! How
redundant! Who wrote this book?!"

"What's a *blaze?*" I asked. I mean—I
always said things like 'Blazes' or 'Oh, my
Blazes', but I never thought a blaze was an
actual, real creature! I'd always just figured
it was a figure of speech.

Bindr cracked the book open again, miraculously back to the same page. "Blazes are monsters found in the nether," he replied. "They blaze ... *ugh* ... like a flame. Silly book." Bindr closed it again with a snap.

I was totally dismayed.

"The nether!" I cried. "How are we going to get there?!"

It was bad enough getting to the Big Village...

The little old lady near us chimed in at that. "Well, youngster, we'll build a portal, then look around for the blazes, kill them, and come back! Of course!"

That gave me a little ping of fear.

Arg. And that could take *forever!*

"Oh, blazes..." I said, feeling silly about the irony.

"Or..." she continued sweetly, "you could go down to the tournament grounds. There's a boy there selling *blaze roundups*. Oh, I've been on several—they're lots of fun!"

Bindr jumped out of his chair, picking the old lady up, swinging her into the air. "Mabel, you're amazing! We'll head down there right away!"

Mabel laughed and hooted in surprise, then tried to compose herself.

"I'm coming with you," she said, panting, out of breath from the twirling. "I *am* the blaze expert, after all."

Jack cocked an eyebrow and looked over at me.

Add a tiny old lady to our group?

Why not...

"You're in!" I said. I turned to Jack. "So how do we get more spider eyes?"

Jack swished an imaginary sword around our table. "We'll have to go *spider hunting*, Ru."

Bindr flipped opened another book and flipped through the pages. "We need an spider eye for *each potion*, so you'll have to kill *a lot* of spiders."

"That'll be fun," I said, drawing concerned looks from everyone. "...*NOT!*" I added. But, I'd have to do whatever I had to do. "So where can we find them?"

Everyone thought for a moment, then looked down at the little old lady again. Maybe she was a spider expert, too...

Mabel the old lady raised on finger and spoke up in her soft voice. "The old fortress on the hill usually has a nice bunch," she said. "My friends and I go up there to make *string* from their webs..."

"Mabel, you're a gem," I said with a smile. She reminded me of my mom; the general soft helpfulness and heaps of wisdom.

I stood to go, anxious to get through the spider killing, when Jack suddenly stopped me.

"Not so fast, Ru," he said. "Now we have a plan for *the potions*. But what about the golden apples?"

"Oh, apples are easy," Bindr said. "I've got a nice tree in my yard."

"And the gold?" Jack replied.

"The tournament..." said the nephew from the across the room, peeking out from behind a bookshelf. I waited for him to elaborate, but he didn't. The young Librarian was terrible at giving complete information.

"What tournament?" I asked.

"The winner gets a bunch of gold," he replied quietly.

Jack looked at me and I looked at Jack. Maybe one of us could win? Jack could win for sure, and I'd at least get some experience fighting! Win and win...

"It's worth a shot," Jack said. Then, "Okay, we have a plan!"

First, we picked up the easy supplies: water bottles, mushrooms, and sugar, then carried them to Bindr's hut, along with all of the books he wanted to borrow for reference.

By then, it was lunchtime, so we stopped for a snack.

"I'm curious—how are you feeling, Ru?" Bindr asked, peering at me intently. "Feeling any effects of the *triple Villager's curse?* Did the time you spent in the Big Village make you want to stay there ... ah ... abnormally?"

I checked myself. "No," I replied. "It's a nice village, but it's not mine. I'm okay."

"Maybe being in a strange village is okay in small doses," the witch said. "We'll keep an eye on you..."

"Okay," I said, looking at Jack, who sat sharpening his sword. "Let's go round up some blazes!"

The soldier smiled and stood.

Jack and I walked to the tournament grounds to meet up with Mabel. Because of a high wall surrounding the area, we couldn't see the actual area where people were going to fight...

I was disappointed. Any advantage I could tell now, before the tournament, would be good.

Since the tournament was in two days, and the village was filled with tourists, there were many people selling their wares outside the arena walls. I saw everything there, from food to rugs to weapons ... but nothing we needed.

Jack, Mabel, and I all wandered around, just to see if anyone *did* have blaze powder or spider eyes for sale, but no one did.

"He's right over there,' Mabel eventually said, pointing. At the end of the grounds, facing a field, was a tall, imposing rectangular frame made of deep, black rock. Stretched across its open interior was a weird, magical field of purple glowing fire.

As we approached, the portal—that *had* to be a nether portal—moaned and vibrated through my whole body...

"Oh, blazes..." I muttered, making eye contact with Jack, who also looked uncomfortable.

"Oh, *yoo-hoo!* Chuck!" called Mabel. "I've brought you some friends."

"Mabel...!" The man the old lady was looking for held out both arms, then took one of Mabel's tiny hands in both of his big hands. He looked down at her with appreciation. "Tis *wonderful* to see you! Are you back again to scare the blazes out of the blazes?" The man named Chuck laughed heartily at his own joke—something he probably said all the time.

"Oh yes," she replied. "We need to kill at least *three* of them. Is that all right?" I watched Mabel haggle with Chuck over the price. It seemed that she wore him down pretty easily.

"No guarantees, of course!" He said with a big—possibly false—smile.

"Of course," she said meekly.

After a small exchange of silver, it was time to step through...

I may be a villager, but I've heard of all kinds of things—including the nether—

and I was totally interested in (and a bit terrified of) seeing another dimension!

Holding my breath when I stepped through the shimmering purple field, I put my hand on my sword, just in case. Would the blazes attack us all at once? Would we have to hunt them down? I was ready for anything...

The Nether was a dark place with glowing red lava fountains, and boy was it hot! I looked around—we were in an open area. There was a building of lava rock nearby, and a line of *villagers*, patiently waiting to get in!

What kind of racket is this? I wondered.

A girl near us announced to everyone, "Make sure you remember which portal you used! Use the same portal when you come back. Not a *different* portal—use the *same portal*..." She spoke as if bored, as if she said that same thing over and over again while she worked. Multiple portals were indeed lined up in a row, and people—young and old—popped in and out every few seconds. We had emerged from one of many.

"Stick to *this one*," whispered Mabel. "Stand in line with me."

Soft music was playing in the background. Another girl was setting out drinks for sale next to little blaze toys with price tags on them.

Eventually, we made it to the front of the lava rock building, and it was our turn to go inside...

Another girl stood near the doorway, and said, "Tickets please." Mabel handed three tickets over. The girl opened a chest, and took out two snowballs. "Creepers!" she said in surprise. "Jolea, go get some more ammunition will ya?" she yelled at the one selling miniature blaze toys. The one named Jolea nodded, put on a coat and stepped through another purple portal. A minute later, she was back—covered in a dusting of snow—with a bucket full of fresh snowballs!

"Sorry you had to wait," the ticket counter said, smiling. "Have an extra snow ball ... on the house." We took our bucket, and stepped inside.

I was expecting to duke it out with strange and terrifying fire creatures on another world, surrounded by flames, lava, and monsters! What we encountered inside that building was quite a shock, and I was really to be blown out of my shoes by a fierce battle! It was sad really. We walked into a dark room full of blazes—odd, floating creatures made of fire and weird, hovering, glowing rods. *Those must be blaze rods*, I thought, peering through the flames. The blazes hardly moved, and were apparently too discouraged to throw fireballs at us. The depressed monsters just *floated in mid-air* while we picked them off. Then, we collected four glowing rods that a fourth girl retrieved without fear, then we left.

"Wasn't that exciting?" Mabel asked, her sweet little face lit up by fire and lava all around us.

I'd never been so disappointed in my life!

Well—at least we had our blaze rods for the powder. When went back to Big Village through the portal—parting ways with Mabel at the library—and eventually returned to Bindr's hut, the witch immediately put the items into his crafting table.

"Good job, Ru and Jack. While you were gone, I organized our things."

Bindr had added new bookcases, and the items were neatly sorted within. One shelf was for the potion components, the other for the apples and gold. Books were stacked on another, and various useful items were organized on a fourth.

This was encouraging. I could see that we had gathered most of what we needed. After a short *spider hunt*—which had to be way easier than going to the Nether to get blaze rods—and winning some gold in the tournament, and we'd be good to go! *Mom and Dad, here I come!* I thought.

I smirked.

How hard could hunting spiders be?

Book 3, Chapter 2

Spiders hunt after dark, and it wasn't dark yet. Getting the blaze rods took barely any time at all—again, disappointing—so Jack and I decided to visit the Big Village Blacksmith.

"Little Smudge, you stay here with Bindr, and we'll be back soon." I told my ocelot. Smudge curled up on a book and was soon snoozing peacefully. No need to worry about her!

"If you're going to be in the tournament," Jack said, "you'd better get some armor. Even a basic *helmet* would be better than nothing."

We didn't have much to trade, but I thought maybe I could do some work for the blacksmith. When we arrived, the old man was trying to work the fire and forge all by himself.

"Hello! " I called out, over the noise of hammering. The poor man was frantically alternating working the bellows, fanning the flame, and running to the other side to hammer. The flames would quickly die out, then he'd start all over again...

"Care to trade some *skilled labor* for armor?" I said, standing next to him.

The old blacksmith looked up at me with one eye, the other busy working.

"What can *you* do?" He grunted.

For an answer, I slipped over to the fire, and soon had it stoked beautifully. His eyes widened in appreciation, and he gave me a strange look. Then, he concentrated on finishing his work.

Jack did nothing. Blazes.

A little while later, the man said, "Okay, switch!" then he took up the fire while I hammered. We were working on a shield. Even though I hadn't had a chance to start my apprenticeship yet back with Dad, a lot of the knowledge had stuck with me. I did a fair job. I worked with the old man for another hour, until the pile of projects was done. It was just in time too, for right when we finished, a man come running up to pick up the new products. *Whew!*

"Thanks," the man said, wiping sweat from his heavy brow. "Who are you? You're obviously a blacksmith, but you're not from around here." He drank a ladleful of water, then handed the makeshift drink to me. Wow, did clean water taste great after working with hot metal!

"I'm *Ru*, son of Cru the Blacksmith."

As soon as I introduced myself, the man dropped his ladle. "Cru!" he exclaimed. "Why—he's a legend! I'm honored to meet you, Ru." The man stuck out one hardened hand, and said, "I'm Patirk. I run this shop with my son, Kriinkle. Did you say you wanted to trade work for armor?"

"Yes," I said, warm and fuzzy inside after hearing that my dad's reputation was so good. "I don't have any goods to trade with, but I have my skills. I need at least a helmet, and a shield would be good, too. "

"I'd be glad to get you some! You helped me in a crisis, my boy, and besides— you're the son of Cru! I'll be right back!"

I stood, and he took a long look at me, then went off into the back. There was rattling in the shop, and pretty soon, Patirk returned with an armful.

"You're big—I think this might fit. Try it on." I looked at the suit of armor he offered me with shock. *If only* it would fit—*blazes!* I put the armor on, piece by piece, and it fit perfectly—helmet, chest plate, leggings, boots and a shield; all shiny, new, durable iron!

"I want you to have it, Ru" Patirk said. "A Knight ordered custom the suit and paid for it, but he never came to pick it up! It's been *years*. I've always wanted to give it to someone special."

I stammered, shaking my head. "But ... I can't take this!" I said, even though I really wanted it. Blazes—the suit of armor made me look like a real warrior! I started

300

to take it off, but the old blacksmith stopped me.

"Please!" he said. "I insist!"

We stared at each other.

Well... I thought. *Who was I to turn it down?*

"Okay, but..." I said, "if you ever need *anything* from me or my family, it's yours. Deal?"

I held out my hand, and he shook it.

"Deal!"

Now I was ready to kill some spiders!

The abandoned fort wasn't far, and Mabel had packed sandwiches. I was so excited about my armor that I kept dancing around Jack—*clang, clatter, clang...*

"Man, you have all the luck," the soldier said. "I'm stuck with this old *creepy* armor..."

"Ha HA!" I laughed—not at him, but out of pure excitement. "Don't worry, Jack! I'll make you some more armor myself, or even better, I'll get *Dad* to do it! At least you *have* armor."

We made it to the old fort, and climbed through the filthy stairs and wreckage to the top. This seemed like a popular place for watching sunsets, since there were fallen bricks all over that had been dragged to form seats and tables.

Jack and I sat and ate, and watched the sun go down. Soon the spiders would come out of hiding!

Since the moon wasn't going to be as bright, we had brought torches with us, and wood to make a campfire. It was chilly, and once we'd built a good fire, we stood by the edge of the flames, and waited...

We waited and waited...

Blazes! I thought. *Where were the spiders?* Soon enough, I was dozing off, full of pleasant thoughts of dad and mom being so amazed and happy with me. My brother

Brew—he'd be astounded, but not surprised...

"I'd better get some more wood," Jack said suddenly, jolting me awake. We had left a pile at the base of the tower.

"Should I come with you?" I yawned.

"Eh ... I got it."

Jack disappeared into the darkness, and I dozed again...

I think I only nodded off for a few minutes, but the next thing I knew, Jack was stumbling back into the firelight. He carried the wood with shaky arms, and his face was white and clammy!

"Ru. Wake up! They're coming!"

One look at Jack's face had me on my feet, sword in hand. My armor gleamed in the torch light.

The thing about spiders is sometimes you feel them—or hear them—before you see them. *Especially* at night, when their dark, hairy bodies blend into the darkness like shadows...

I heard their scratchy claws first, then I could feel them crawling up the outside walls of the fort through the floor! When I turned, I could see their low bodies slinking along the stones. The big arachnids came in from the walls, the stairway—even the tower behind us—surrounding us, but staying *out* of the firelight.

"I ... uh .... think we *underestimated* the amount of spiders..." Jack whispered.

"Blazes—yeah!" I replied, keeping my back to his.

As if on a cue, the creatures hissed and attacked!

Now—I've gotta tell you: *armor is amazing!* With one hand, I used my sword, and with the other, my shield, which I also used as a weapon. My training as a blacksmith came in handy; I could smite (hit hard) with either hand!

My legs and chest were protected, so I just waded into the flurry of bristly legs and scratchy, dark bodies and clicking fangs and hacked! I hacked and hacked and bashed with my shield!

"Doing okay, Jack?" I yelled.

"Okay here!" Jack shouted back.

"Look at *all* those spider eyes!" I exclaimed. "*Yippee!*"

"It's a treasure trove!"

In time, the spiders began to thin out, and I was glad for it! Even my arms—as strong as they were from banging away horseshoes all day—were tired. One last arachnid scuttled away as dawn was breaking...

When the fort was quiet again, and we were left standing in a pile of dead spider parts, Jack and I both laughed.

"We did it!!" I exclaimed, then began scooping up spider eyes and string. Jack did the same.

"Bindr can use the *extras* to open his shop and—"Jack began to say. His sentence was cut off by a surprised cry. "Ruuuuuuu!"

I turned swiftly, dropping a gross eyeball. Jack was being carried off by two nasty spiders!

Drawing my sword again, I chased after them, pausing in midstride to grab a couple of torches.

Might need these! I thought.

The spiders crawled down the wall, and I raced down the stairs after them. I was just in time to see the arachnids carry Jack kicking and screaming into a dark hole in the wall. *Yikes!*

Rushing up, I began tearing away fallen bricks, then noticed with a shot of fear that it wasn't a hole—it was a cave.

Cave spiders!

I had no choice. I had to rescue my friend! I followed Jack and his kidnappers down into the cave. The dark tunnel—full of spider webs—went down and down, and as it descended, it gradually opened up into a wide cavern...

My torch seemed very, very small.

I was just one little point of light in all that darkness...

"Jack!" I yelled, my voice echoing. "Make some noise so I can follow you!"

Jack began clanking his heels on the ground, and that helped a lot. I followed the sound, desperate to catch up.

TWANNNGGG!

I heard something crunch into the stone close to me. Looking down, I saw an arrow.

What?!

TWANNNGGG!

It was another, and that one almost hit me! I began to duck and weave as I ran on after Jack...

The torch was making me a perfect target, but there was *no way* I was going to drop my light source! I'd go from target to dinner in no time.

Bursting into another cavern full of stone and mud, I suddenly saw Jack, wrapped up in cobwebs, lying at the feet of a skeleton archer who was—crazily enough—riding a spider!

There was no time to question. I just had to get Jack, and fast!

The cavern was filled with blue-black spiders. One of the arachnids smiled at me, and I saw poison dripping from its fangs...

As my eyes widened in horror, I felt something hard hit me—BAM—in the chest! Looking down, I saw another arrow, its shaft and feathers sticking out of my chest plate. If I wasn't wearing this armor, I'd be a dead man.

I felt a red-hot fury rise in me like the fuming bellows of my family's forge, and I *snapped*.

"Oh no, you don't!" I shouted, and started throwing everything I could at the Skeleton, starting with the rocks at my feet! I put the lit torch down on the stony floor, and there was plenty of glowing red light with which to see my target.

I drove the skeleton jockey back. Every time the jerk tried to shoot an arrow at me, I slammed it with a rock. Finally, I knocked the monster off of a ledge, but not before it looked at me with black, empty eye sockets, and hissed, "You and me! Some time... Someplace..."

"Anytime!" I bellowed back at the skeleton and his spider mount as the last rock hurtled them both over the cliff. The skeleton and spider fell, hopefully to their deaths in the intestines of the world...

I stared out into the black, huffing and puffing, then dropped the rock in my hand.

Shaking my head, I wondered why I didn't just use my sword. I was so used to throwing horseshoes...

"Uh, Ru?"

Jack was at my feet.

"Yeah, Jack?"

"Can you ... um ... untie me *quickly?* The spiders are coming..."

Oh blazes! Did I kill their leader?! Now they wanted revenge!

With one quick and careful swipe of my trusty sword, Jack was free. We ran back toward the fallen torch, scooping it up. Something else that didn't belong on the cave floor caught my eye on the ground next to it, and scooped it up as well, determined to look at whatever it was later.

Dodging out of the way of some oncoming very angry spiders, Jack and I ran around a boulder and turned off of the path. Before we could take two more steps, we were suddenly wrapped up in cobwebs.

315

My sword was out, but I could barely move my arm. We had fallen into their trap!

"Jack! What can we do?" I gasped as I struggled to move.

"Burn it!" He screamed back, even though we were both stuck in the same spot. His shout shook my ears.

Good idea! I thought. As I wriggled the torch in a circle around us, the webs immediately began to burn in little flyway strings. Pretty soon I had burned a hole in the trap, and the two of us were free again! Well—sort of. Actually, we were still deep underground with angry spiders trying to kill us, and who knows what the blazes was out there! But it felt good to be able to move again...

After that, it was just run back up the way we came as fast as we possibly could! We miraculously managed to stay ahead of the spiders, and I handed one torch to Jack as I lit the other—we tried to keep a wide circle of light around us.

It was daylight up on the surface. I could see the entrance to the cave approaching, letting in the light...

But just as we started to get close to our exit, the ceiling began to move...

I stopped in my tracks, and clutched at Jack's arm. "What ... is that?!" I could barely get the words out—my throat was gripped with terror!

"BB...B..B..B Bats!" the soldier replied, eyes wide and white in the darkness.

The creatures descended on us, swirling all around us, shrieking so loudly that my ears were shrieking back!

"Yuck!" Jack shouted. "Don't let them fly in your mouth!" He ran for the entrance.

Bats are disgusting! I thought. I felt like I was being battered by ten thousand scoldings.

But at last ... we made it out.

"Hooray!" I yelled, and of course, one bat took the opportunity to fly into my mouth. *YUCK!*

Jack led the way up the staircase. I was so tired and disgusted that I couldn't make my legs work right...

We gathered up all of our things the camp we'd made on top of the fort, made sure that the fire was out, and retrieved all of the spider eyes and string.

"Let's leave the torches," Jack said, "in case anyone else needs them."

"Yeah, okay."

We made our weary way home— back to Bindr's hut—sore but triumphant...

Book 3, Chapter 3

What a long night. And we didn't sleep!

After a couple of cups of coffee, I felt a lot better. Bindr made an egg and bacon omelet—which was delicious—and he didn't mind making another when I asked.

The shelves were looking pretty good. The potion bookcase was full. We had enough ingredients to make plenty.

My beautiful armor was standing next to the shelves on a makeshift armor stand. I decided that I'd spend some time cleaning and polishing it up before the start of the tournament. Spider blood and cobwebs were stuck all over it.

Bindr and Smudge had stayed up until the wee hours studying. Smudge was drinking coffee too.

"One thing we found out," Bindr said, "is that if we want to throw the potion onto your parents, Ru, instead of trying to make them drink it, we'd better make a *splash* potion. We'll need gunpowder for that..."

"Splashing sounds a lot easier than handing them a drinking glass." I replied. "So how do we get gunpowder?"

Bindr tapped the book that sat open on the table. "*Creepers*. When you kill them. But you have to kill creepers from a distance, or *you'll* get blown up instead."

"Bow and arrow?" asked Jack.

"That's an idea," I replied. I had practiced some with a bow and a target back when I was secretly training before this whole mess began. "Is there a particular place where creepers hang out around Big Village?"

"Well," Binder said, stroking his chin. "There is, in fact, a place they call *Creeper Canyon*." Man—Bindr knew everything! "The creepers come up from the caves, and if we let them out of the canyon, they just wander right into the village!"

"Oh good," Jack said. "So if we kill those creatures to get some gunpowder, we'll also be helping the village?"

Bindr shrugged with the faintest bit of a cackling sound, then turned back to his book.

Helping the village would be great. It was a good point—not like snowballing those poor blazes. I smiled at Jack.

"Haven't you two been out all night?" Binder asked, cocking his heavy brow. "Aren't you tired?"

"Eh," I replied. The coffee really helped. I felt fine, at the moment.

"I'm good," Jack replied. "But I'll be sleeping hard tonight—that's for sure..."

"Jack," I said, moving toward my armor stand. "Let's go get some gunpowder..."

Later, Jack and I were lying down at the edge of the canyon, looking peering over the landscape. The canyon was pretty shallow at our end, and we could see that at the other end of the big, sandy rift was a big cave entrance.

The canyon was built like a ramp, pointing right up at toward Big Village.

There were *lots* of creepers moseying around, generally heading up toward town.

"So explain to me again," Jack said, "*why exactly* you said that we don't need a bow and arrows? I mean—if that's true, then it's good, because we don't have any..."

"Ever play horseshoes?" I asked.

A light dawned on Jack's face. "Like ... the spiders you killed in our first fight with them! Oh yeah..."

I pulled out a pile of horseshoes. We'd have to run down there to retrieve them, which could be dangerous. But that just added to the fun, didn't it?

We took position, each with a clutch of heavy iron horseshoes.

Whenever a creeper wandered into our range, we'd each throw a shoe, taking turns. After a few hits, hissing and glaring around to figure out where it was being attacked from, BAM—the creeper would die before blowing itself up, and there'd be a nice little pile of gunpowder.

Every once and a while, when Jack or I ran out of ammo, whoever was out would run down to gather the flung horseshoes and piles of gunpowder, and the other stood guard.

It was totally fun!

Not much later, Jack and I returned to Binder's hut, laughing and talking.

"Did you see that one's expression on that one by the bush right before my horseshoe hit him in the head?! Ha ha..."

"Yeah, and those two ran right into each other and killed each other. Nice!"

Bindr met us at the door with a big smile.

"Got gunpowder?"

"Yep," we both said together, grinning broadly.

"Good job, boys!"

While we were gone, Bindr had apparently rearranged the bookcases, and now, there was an area for general potion supplies as well. The special place waiting for *potion of weakness* ingredients was stacked with empty bottles waiting to be filled. The *potions of healing* Bindr had received with his brewing kit were also stacked aside in their own area as well.

The brewing stand and crafting station had been moved to a table by the window.

On a pillow on the table was Smudge, who was curled up napping when we returned. My ocelot pal woke, stretched, and rose up to greet us. I scratched her head, and she purred and rubbed against me. "We're doing *good things*, Smudge. Not too long from now, we'll have everything we need."

"That reminds me!" said Jack. "We'd better sign up for the tournament. We have until sundown, but let's get it done now so we don't forget!"

"Good idea," I replied. "We're outta here. Bye!"

I was excited. It was time to find out about the tournament...

When we reached the tournament gates—which were still closed—Jack and I came across a man standing by with a book and quill. A short line of fighters waited to sign up. Most of the men were puny farmers, or overweight bakers, but there were a couple of guys that looked like professional soldiers. I could tell, because they stood with an sort of ... *alertness*— eyes constantly scanning—oh, and they were wearing armor and weapons.

One of the hard dudes—a small man in black with chainmail—was soon closely watching Jack. Jack of course, looked like a great fighter, wearing full armor and standing tall with confidence.

No one noticed me, it seemed. It was funny. *If only they knew!* My goofy appearance was a weapon in itself...

A baker at the front of the line replied loudly to something the man with the book said with, "Are you crazy? *NO!*" then stomped off.

Weird, I thought.

When it was finally my turn to sign up, and I told the man my name. He said, "If you fight in the tournament, you agree to accept all responsibility for any maiming, damage or trauma received or given. Say yes or no."

"Yes," I said, confidently.

"And in the event of your death, it's your own fault and no one else's. Say yes or no."

Yes," I repeated, but not as strongly.

"And you agree to use *no* armor, weapons or potions of any kind, except for those provided to you, and *if you do anyway*, you'll be immediately kicked out of placement and ridiculed for cheating! Say yes or no..."

Now I understood the baker's reaction.

I had no choice. And it made sense to disallow outside gear. At the very least, everyone would have an even chance...

"Yes," I said again, and signed an *X* by my name when the man offered me the quill.

I was in the tournament ... as a warrior!

"No armor?!" We were back and the hut, and Jack was very upset. "How am I gonno fight without armor or weapons? This totally sucks eggs!" He pounded his fist on Bindr's table.

I was not about to let him get psych'd out. "Yeah, but you're a great fighter, Jack!" I exclaimed. "And you've had all that training and experience—way more than me! You can win bare handed if you had to!"

"Well, I believe in you," Bindr said to the soldier. Smudge jumped up onto the table and licked Jack's hand.

"Hand-to-hand combat is *completely different* than fighting with weapons," Jack said. "It's been years since I did any of that kind of training. Ru ... honestly, I think *you* have a better chance at this."

Actually—up until then—I'd been thinking that Jack would win the tournament, and I'd be happy to just get a little practice in. I never actually considered that winning the gold would be up to *me*...

"Gulp." I said.

"You'd better get used to being without your armor," Bindr said to Jack. "How about you take it off? Let's put it next to Ru's."

"Gulp," Jack said too. "Okay..."

I quickly built a little armor stand while Jack removed his sooty-black plate mail. When the soldier was finished, he stood next to his evil-looking armor standing on the wooden frame, and said, "I feel *different* without it."

Jack looked different too. Smaller. Cleaner.

"What an interesting metal..." said Bindr. "I'll have to research it sometime. Now, let's all go practice!"

"Hand-to-hand combat is really personal," Jack said, slapping me lightly on the face.

"Hey!" I replied, slightly insulted.

"See?" Jack exclaimed. "Isn't it awful?" He was trying not to laugh.

We were standing in the field just outside Bindr's hut, and the sunshine felt good on my skin. A few rabbits hopped around in the grass nearby.

I punched Jack in the arm in response.

"Ouch!" he said, and I laughed out loud. Jack rubbed his arm. "And we're not even trying to *hurt each other*. In a *real* combat, you get knocked down, get blackened eyes, and blood squirts everywhere!"

Yuck.

"So how do we practice without us killing each other?"

"Healing potions," Jack replied. "Let's go hard, and after we're done, we'll heal ourselves. Otherwise, we'd have to wait until our natural healing kicks in, which can be hours or days depending on how badly we're hurt."

Sweet! "Okay, let's do it!"

Jack and I punched, dodged, grabbed, slapped, tripped and whatever else we could think of, until we were each an oozing, sore mess...

"Good work, Ru!" Jack exclaimed through a swollen jaw. I had no idea how he was still being so cheerful with us each being so beaten up. "You totally held your own! You're very strong!"

"Thanks, Jack," I grumbled, limping on both legs back to the hut. "You're a good teacher."

I hurt all over, but had learned a lot! When we first started, I was mostly concerned with not being hit. But it seemed that focusing on hitting the other guy was more important. Jack taught me to avoid being hit if possible, but not to fear it. The fear ties you up...

When we returned inside the hut, Bindr was just pulling a new potion out of the brewer.

"How did it go?" the novice witch asked, setting the glass vial down onto the table.

"Great," I replied, trying to smile through a swollen lip. "I'm going to get cleaned up, then maybe I can take a healing potion?" I looked around for Smudge. *Where was that cat?* Maybe she was out hunting?

"I'll get some healing potions ready for you two." Bindr replied without moving. He was working.

Jack and I washed up, then went back and sat at the table.

"So, how's your potion practice going, Bindr?" I asked. I was feeling more and more sore by the minute. Everything was tightening up.

'Hee hee—just fine," Bindr cackled, rocking back and forth a little in his chair.

Was it my imagination, or was he a little ... *greener* than this morning? *It must be the blows to my head*, I decided.

"I started to research the metal your armor is made from, Jack," Bindr said, tapping his chest. He had put the chest plate on. "I hope you don't mind, but I put it on to observe its properties. The material is very mysterious. *Tingly*."

"I don't mind," Jack replied politely. "Let's get those potions, please...?"

Two bottles of magical fluid were on the table. I pick one up and handed it to Jack.

"This must be them..."

As soon as I drank mine, I knew that something was wrong...

Instead of feeling back to normal, I felt a hundred times worst! I looked at Jack, and he was clutching at his chest.

We'd been poisoned!

"Bindr!" I croaked. "Help! I don't feel good. There's something ... wrong with—"

"Hee hee hee, *of course* you don't, Ru!" Bindr replied with a cackle, hopping up and down in glee. "I've been practicing my *potions*, you see..."

"What have you done, witch?!" Jack gasped as he sank down to the floor. The bruises I had given him in practice grew and crawled across his skin, black against his white face instead of merely blue.

Bindr didn't respond. Instead, he turned away from the brewing stand and watched us with an evil glint in his eye. "Did you know that a *potion of harming* is nothing more than a *potion of healing* brewed with a fermented spider's eye?"

I stared at him in horror.

We'd been poisoned ... by Bindr! He was turning *bad!*

Getting out a book and quill, Bindr began taking notes, looking at us and saying, "mmm hmmm—interesting response, or *lack* thereof..."

We were his experiment!

"Jack," I croaked. "Bindr's losing himself and turning into a witch! What do we do?" I clutched at the table to keep myself from falling onto the floor like Jack had. My ears were roaring, and I couldn't breathe...

"Something must have ... happened to him while we were gone!" Jack replied with a struggle. "What's different?" Jack crawled over to me, too weak to stand.

Where was Smudge? My ocelot was nowhere to be seen...

"Bindr, did you do something to my cat?!" I demanded as strongly as I could.

"Don't be ridiculous," Bindr replied with a wry smile. "I would *never* harm a cat! Smudge began hissing at me and went outside. But she'll get used to the *new me*, eventually." Bindr pondered and made a note. "I should *track* how long it takes her!"

Jack pulled himself to his knees next to me, using my chair and the table. "Armor," he muttered. "It must be my armor!" he hissed in my ear. "We've got to get it off of him!"

Of course!

"Alright, Jack," I said, bracing myself. "One, two, three, now GO!" I breathed, and together, we did our best to grab Bindr, stumbling at him with clumsy arms, trying not to fall down. Jack flung himself against Bindr's legs, holding him down. Bindr was too shocked to move, so I summoned all my strength, then leaned and pulled the chest plate over his head as the witch screamed and struggled! When the chest plate broke free, I flung it into a corner of the hut.

"Quick—is that the only armor he's wearing?!" Jack asked frantically as Bindr struggled against the soldier's weakened grasp. Either Bindr was unexpectedly strong from carrying all those books, or we were terribly weak from the potion, but both of us—working together—could barely hold!

I searched the witch's body as best I could without letting him get away.

There was no more armor.

"Now what?!" I asked. By this time, Bindr was sprawled out on the table, and I was sitting on his back and Jack was holding down his legs. Smudge suddenly strolled in through the window, and sat on Bindr's head, then turned and hissed at the armor.

"Let's tie him up and get the armor away from him!"

"Okay..."

I could barely feel my natural strength starting to return, so I quickly gathered some rope, and we tied Bindr to a chair. The witch responded by trying to kill us with evil glances.

Are his eyes turning red? I wondered, but I couldn't quite tell.

Jack rummaged through the shelves for the label marked *Potions of Healing*. "Bindr?" Jack asked, holding up a glass vial full of red goop. "Is this *actual* potion of healing, or did you switch everything around, like a sneaky witch?"

Bindr refused to speak, closing his mouth in a firm line while throwing eye daggers...

"Maybe Smudge will be able to tell," I said. I poured some of the red stuff into a saucer, and Smudge drank it eagerly, then leapt from the table to the top of a bookcase in one healthy bound.

"Traitor!" Bindr spat, looking up at Smudge, who licked her paw and cleaned her face.

It looked good.

Hoping for the best, I took one tiny sip, and immediately felt better. I drank a couple of gulps, then handed the bottle to Jack. We were cured!

Not long after that—with both Jack and I back to normal—I gathered up all of the pieces of Jack's black-gold armor, and took the suit outside. At the edge of Bindr's garden was a little potting shed. I locked the armor pieces in there, hoping that the weird metal wouldn't kill any surrounding plants.

When I returned, Bindr was already looking better...

"Do we give him a healing potion?" Jack asked.

"I don't know," I replied, staring at Bindr's confused face. "Would it heal him back to the real Bindr, or back to being a healthy witch?"

"What if he never changes all the way back?" Jack asked worriedly. "What if this transformation is one way, and the Bindr we knew is gone...?"

A chill ran up my spine.

There was no way to know, or to tell, so Jack and I let time do its work. As the evening went on, it seemed that Bindr was becoming more and more of his old self. Of course, since witches are crafty and evil, we didn't bother listening to Bindr asking us to untie him, saying he was now completely cured. It was only when *Smudge* went over and rubbed against Bindr's body, purring, that we decided to let him go...

The novice witch didn't really remember what had happened to him, and it wasn't until we showed him the notes that *evil Bindr* wrote in the book that he fully believed us. Then, he was devastated!

"I could have killed you two! I *do* remember wanting to hurt you, but it was like ... like a dream!"

"Well, we learned more about the armor at least," I said, patting Bindr on the head kindly. "It makes evil eviler."

"And turn good people mean," Jack said shivering. "I can't believe I used to wear it *all the time*..."

"See?" I replied, clapping Jack on his unarmored arm. "Everything worked out!"

I wanted to be optimistic—especially for Bindr. But I was going to keep a close eye on that witch, and if he started turning green again, I'd have to act fast!

"Dinner...?" Bindr asked meekly, hoping to clear the air.

We laughed.

"Sure!"

Book 3, Chapter 4

After a quiet night of rest and recuperation, I woke up ready the day. In fact, I wasn't just ready—I was *totally excited!*

Today was the tournament!

My first tournament! I thought with a grin. *Wow!* If anyone asked me a week ago, I would never in a million setting suns say that I'd be fighting in a warrior tournament *today*.

After our coffee and bread, Jack and I went through some warm up stretches. Up, down, twist; making sure that all our muscles were ready. Then, we *mentally* stretched. Ready to win? Yes! Imagining all that gold? Yes!

As Jack and I prepared for the competition, Bindr and Smudge practiced their cheering, and before long, we were ready to fight...

Just to be safe, I double-locked the potting shed and took the key with me. For all we knew, that evil armor might be irresistible to anyone passing by, calling out with the sweet sounds of power...

We all arrived at to the tournament grounds and I saw that the gates were open. *Huzzah* as they say. Walking inside with the others, I took a look around. Mabel was already there, waiting with a group of her friends. All of the old women carried flags that said, 'Go Ru' or 'Go Jack.'

I smiled. We had an *old lady cheering squad!*

The fighting area was large, fenced-in arena with benches stacked all around. Smaller arenas were setup as well so that people could wander between them, stand and watch their favorites, or go to the snack booth and get a cool drink.

Smudge rode on Bindr's shoulder, completely at ease. The contestants were waiting at the far end of the grounds, so Jack and I said goodbye and walked over together. A lot of people had signed up to fight—I couldn't even see who all was there!

The man who had signed me up yesterday was addressing everyone.

"Time for the Rules," he said, waving Jack and I in closer. "Now, this is very simple! *Everyone fights*. If you lose, you're out. If you cheat, you're out. If you *win*, you keep going, being paired up against other winners, until only one victor remains! *That* person gets the gold." He paused, looking around at the murmuring group of contestants, then went on. "To win a round, the other person has to give up, or be unconscious. For each round, *we* will give you instructions and issue weapons, if any. Is everyone ready?"

Several people cheered in the affirmative. Others looked around at all of the other contestants, groaning and mumbling.

"Ready!" Jack and I shouted simultaneously.

The man spoke up again. "Come on people—we're putting on a show! Let's see some *spirit!* Now *are you ready?!*" This time, everyone growled, yelled or whooped, and the man smiled. "Now *that's* more like it. Keep it up! Now, let's get this going..."

We were all broken up into groups, and I was assigned to one of the smaller arenas, and was up first. As I waited for direction, a man handed me a long stick with a pillow tied to it. My opponent was a younger boy with a long pony tail. The kid looked terrified.

"Attention, attention!" the referee shouted. I looked around, and saw all of the arenas set up with fighters ready to go, just as I was. "Round one is about to begin! Everyone, let's hear some noise!"

The crowd was definitely into it. I had a few people watching me, along with Bindr, Smudge and some of Mabel's group. Jack was in another arena not far from where I was, and I saw that the man who we saw in line yesterday at sign-up—the dark-clothed soldier in chainmail—in another.

"And now ... BEGIN!"

I turned toward my opponent, who promptly threw down his pillow stick down into the dirt and fled. The crowd *booed*.

Yay! I thought, grinning. *I won my first fight!*

Later, after watching others battle for a while, I decided to wander around and see how Jack was doing. Jack had won his first match easily, smacking his opponent with the pillow until he cried. The dark soldier—that's what we were calling that small guy in chainmail who's been eying Jack yesterday—had also won his. This was pretty exciting.

With a little time left until the second round, I wandered around to watch more of the first *pillow-stick* matches. The sights and sounds were thrilling. Even the *smell* was great: fresh food, hay, sweat, and candy...

And then I smelled something horribly familiar.

Could that be Smelly? I wondered, frantically looking around. Was it one of the bullies that I had punched because he was burning Smudge's tail?

And then I saw the brute. *On no!* He was in the tournament, and there were Biggest and Loudest—his evil friends—cheering him on!

"Jack! Jack!" I shouted, running to find him. The soldier was talking to Bindr, and they both turned to face my frantic approach with shocked faces. "Listen!" I cried. "The Bullies are here!"

Jack knew exactly who I meant. Smudge hissed.

My friend ducked down and glanced around. "I should have known they'd be here!" he said. "Sir Darwym actually likes his men to fight in tournaments, as long as they win. It makes his reputation stronger." Jack's easy confidence vanished.

"I hope I don't have to fight them!" I said. Now I was really worried. The last time I saw those brutes, I'd punched them out up at the hunting camp in the mountains. Since I was just a *lowly villager*, they'd surely have something to prove—not to mention whatever nastiness their boss had ordered them to do if they ever found Jack and me again!

"Ru, I'm don't want to fight them either. They're gonna be *out for blood* since

I ran off." Jack paced up and down anxiously. "I defected!"

"Well, you two can't call it off," said Bindr. "We *need* that gold. You'll just have to do your best!"

"Our best not to get killed," I mumbled, and wondered how I was going to get through the day alive...

My next match was a hand-to-hand fight—no weapons—and I easily beat my opponent. I didn't feel good about hitting the guy, but had decided to do my best to take him out quickly. With just three blows, I knocked him into the fence, and my opponent was waving his hands in surrender.

So yay—I won again. Despite my impending doom, I allowed myself to enjoy the small victory.

But the third match ... was against Loudest.

"YOU!" the bully yelled, which was very loud of course. "I'm gonna tear you LIMB FROM LIMB!!" A crowd gathered excitedly. This was going to be a good show!

"Hey, man, I'm *sorry* about the other day" I said. "I like cats, and I didn't *want* to hit you..." Let's see if another apology would work...

"I will BREAK EVERY BONE IN YOUR BODY!" Loudest screamed. Loudly.

"Come now," I replied, trying to talk smoothly. "Hey—you look fabulous without your armor!" I tried flattering him.

"You will RUE THIS DAY!"

The crowd cheered wildly.

Oh man—there was nothing to do but fight him. Wooden swords were the weapons chosen for this round, and Loudest immediately charged at me, sword held high in the air, ready to plonk me on the head!

"RAAWWWRR!!' he bellowed, running at me like a rhino!

I stepped aside and stuck my foot out. Loudest tripped, and went flying headfirst into the fence, disqualified.

"Winner!" the judge shouted. "Ru the Blacksmith!"

Yay? I thought, watching the steaming brute pull himself back to his feet. His face was red. If this was a victory, I'd take it.

The number of contestants was getting smaller. Jack was still in the running, and so was the chain-mailed soldier that had caught my eye. Loudest complained about my win to the judge, but the judge responded with, "You were knocked unconscious. Your opponent was the winner." Loudest denied it, and I didn't really remember the noisy brute quieting down at all, but in the end, the win held. *Whew!*

If I could last five more rounds, then I would be the winner!

There was a long break, where the remaining contestants were served cold lamb and potatoes. A dance troupe performed for the crowd, and some people could flip and roll! An amateur archery event entertained everyone, especially when the loser got a pie in the face. Jack, Bindr, and I spent a few minutes catching up on what we'd seen separately so far.

"Oh Blazes!" Jack said laughing hysterically. "I wish I could have seen that fight with Loudest! He's gonna hate you forever, Ru!"

"Yep," I replied. "At least that long. So how are you doing Jack?" Jack had a beautiful black eye.

"Good," the soldier replied. "I wish I could use a healing potion, but I'll live..."

"That *dark soldier* you two are watching is doing well too," Bindr said. "And the men you guys call *Smelly* and *Bigger* are still in too." The witch was keeping tabs on the competition for us in between writing notes in a book. "On the bright side, Ru, the odds against you winning are *one hundred to one!* I placed a bet. If you win, we'll have fresh bread for a year!"

Great, I thought. *More pressure...*

"Nice!" Jack added cheerfully. "We'll just do one match at a time, and see what happens."

When the fighting started again, I suddenly didn't feel as confident.

The competition was starting to get better as the weak contestants were weeded out. I barely beat my next opponent, who was long limbed and fast. Luckily, my strength saved me a couple of times, and I won the round.

Yay again. But I was getting tired.

But Jack—he had to fight the dark soldier. I couldn't tell what the two of them were talking about, but it looked like the small man *knew* Jack. At the end, my friend was knocked out, and the dark soldier won the match...

It was all up to me now.

I was standing with the weight of the world on my shoulders—the fate of my parents and my village—when Mabel walked up smiling. "You're doing great, Ru! Don't give up—you're just getting *forged!*"

Mabel was right, and her words warmed my heart.

I was like an iron weapon in the flames   of the forge, getting pounded. Becoming stronger...

In the next round, the dark soldier and Biggest were matched against each other. Unbelievably, Biggest lost, which meant that the dark soldier was even more skilled than I thought.

Meanwhile, I fought a real hard case, and at one point, he had me in a chokehold. I almost lost consciousness, but in the last second, I was able to bang the back of my head against the man's face, and knocked him out. The crowd really loved that.

Smelly won his round, and I heard the brute's opponent complaining about his odor—saying that Smelly had an unfair advantage. But the judge said that it wasn't against the rules. "If his smelly feet can knock you out, you're still out!"

Then, it was my turn to fight the dark soldier!

Jack stepped up to me right before the match started, and whispered, "He's weaker on his left side! Good luck, Ru..."

This was a colored wooden dagger fight. Our edgeless blade had been dipped in *berry juice*, and would leave a mark wherever they hit. Each *mark* counted as a point. The person with the most points by the end ... well ... *lost*.

When the match started, the small-framed dark soldier and I circled each other slowly. I watched the man's mid-section closely to see if I could tell when and where he was going to move...

There! I dodged out of the way as he lashed in at me with his juice-covered dagger, then I struck back.

Again! I swiveled as the dark soldier attacked, then I threw the blade into my left hand to change up my tactic. I kept switching hands and doing weird things with my feet. In the end, I managed to beat the dark soldier by ONE POINT!

Yay!

As I sat, panting and basking in the victory I felt, Jack walked over with a broad grin and brought me a cool drink.

We were almost there...

Finally, it was the last round.

Of course, it was between me ... and Smelly.

The winner of this match would win the entire tournament, the gold, and possibly a year of fresh bread. The odiferous brute and I stood in the central, big arena, and the crowd around us was loud and huge...

Smelly was the meanest of the three bullies, and part of me was really afraid of him. It is one thing to fight someone in a sense of fair play, but Smelly had no honor. No fairness.

We were each given a sword and a shield ... and no armor. I knew that if I failed, then Smelly would likely kill me out of spite, and my cause would be lost. Mom and Dad would be stuck as zombies forever, and my village would be doomed...

The match began, and I tried to quell my fear with the idea that I was a *red-hot iron sword*, quenched and hissing from the oil bath, ready to be carried into battle...

When the leader of the bullies and I clashed, the fight was intense. Smelly was very aggressive, and kept hitting me with both the sword and the shield. *Bang! Bash! Bang!* Every time the brute slammed into me, a wave of stench rolled off of him—not just his *farts* (which he timed with his attacks)—but ripe and putrid *body odor!*

But every time I started to gag, I thought of Mom and Dad, waiting for me to save them. Their zombie eyes in my mind kept me going...

I got in some good strikes—slipping around the Smelly's shield—and I could tell by the hatred in his eyes that I'd hurt him. As we fought on and on, I slammed him with my shield and tried to bite him with my sword, and our bodies and meager protection clashed again and again. Amidst the terrible smell of my opponent, I also heard a flurry of sounds of our struggles: grunts, cries of pain, growls, the breaking of glass—the usual battle sounds.

Just then, Smelly landed a solid blow to my head that I didn't have the strength to block—luckily with the flat of the blade— then another! The world started to swim. *Was he toying with me?!* I would not give up! I felt something damp, and I realized that I was so exhausted that I was crying!

But I kept on and on, blocking as Smelly slammed me again and again, being crushed further and further down into the dirt, until I heard the judge's voice call out for Smelly to stop.

"Contestants, STOP!" he shouted. "Cease fighting!" I realized that his words were echoing weirdly in my head, and my vision was swimming. I was on the ground...

I had lost.

Was I dead? I wondered, but then my vision cleared and I could see the sky again. I caught a glimpse of Smelly's ugly face scowling at me, and his stench drifted along the breeze into my nose as he turned and stomped away.

I was devastated. I sat on the ground in defeat, too tired and shattered to get up. Jack and Bindr came over to console me.

"You did so well, Ru! You almost did it!" Jack said. "We'll find another way— Smelly is a super-strong fighter!"

Bindr spoke up, "Why is your face wet, Ru? And your shirt?

"Tears of sadness," I mumbled. "Tears of loss. I'm a loser..."

"No ... wait a minute! Hey Judge!" Bindr shouted. "Come over here!"

My friends and the judge stood over me, looking me over. Bindr spoke quietly with the man, who peered at my shirt and my tears of shame.

"Ah ... interesting," said the judge. He called the other judges over. They wandered a short distance away, then stood in a huddle talking quietly.

"What's happening?" I asked. My lips were tripping over themselves—why was I so woozy??

"It's okay, Ru," Jack said, crouching down with one hand on my shoulder. "Hang on..."

The judges walked over with stern faces. "Give us your shirt," one of them said, so I took my shirt off and handed it to him. I didn't even care what they were doing.

I looked over across the arena, and saw Smelly was doing a victory pose in the middle of the ring, surrounded by cheering and laughing members of the audience. Biggest and Loudest were with him. I heard Loudest laughing obnoxiously over the noise. A judge strode over and spoke with Smelly, and immediately the brute began protesting and arguing.

The long and the short of it was: Smelly had cheated by throwing a *potion of weakness* on me!

The judges found a second bottle of the stuff in Smelly's clothing, and shards of the first in the dirt where we had been fighting. Furious and arguing loudly, Smelly was disqualified from the tournament for cheating, which meant...

I WON THE TOURNAMENT!

Book 3, Chapter 5

The gold for the golden apples sat on the shelf in Bindr's hut.

That was gold that I had won. Me!

I was all smiles. "I just can't believe it!" I kept saying to Smudge, who was sitting on my lap kneading at my leg.

"Have a healing potion," said Jack, whose black eye was rapidly changing from black to purple to yellow. He handed me a bottle of red goo.

"I don't need one!" I replied. "I feel fantastic! No offense to your potions, Binder..."

It was true. I did feel amazing. I had done it! I won! *Wooooo!*

"No offense taken, Ru." Bindr replied with a quaint smile, rubbing his hands together gleefully. "I'll finish making the *golden apples* tonight! Then, we'll load up in the morning, and go back to your village, Ru. In a few days, you'll be home, and we'll be curing your folks!"

I grinned in response, and ate some bread.

Home.

Most of time during this adventure, I had been able to keep myself busy and not think about Mom and Dad being zombies, or Brew dealing with it back home all this time. Now that we'd done everything we needed to do, I was thinking about my family all the time!

"Jack, what are you going to do about your armor?" I asked. It was mostly to distract myself.

Bindr looked at Jack with concern and added, "Now, I don't know if it would affect me if I was near it or not, but do whatever you want to do. Just keep an eye on me. I don't want to put you two in *danger* again..."

"I never want to touch that armor again," Jack said with a shudder. "Maybe sometime we can find a way to get rid of it.

Ru *has* promised me some new armor after all, haven't you Ru?"

"For sure," I said. I, on the other hand, would be wearing my new iron armor. I smiled, imaging my brother Brew's face when he saw me pull up in a full suit of iron armor! And when I told my brother about all our adventures...? He'd be astounded!

I wanted to leave right then, but we had hours of sleeping and preparations in the way...

Little old Mabel saw us off in the morning, giving us loads of nice things to carry with us on the journey.

"Goodbye," she said sweetly, coming and giving each of us a tiny but heartfelt hug. "I'll look after your hut and your plants Bindr—don't you worry..."

"Thanks, Mabel. Don't mess around with my potions or brewing stand!"

Mabel looked shocked. "I would never! Maybe I'd have a small card game or tea party there, but don't worry about it! Run along now."

Jack, Bindr and I started off, walking down through the Big Village, Smudge riding inside my shirt.

Since I'd won the tournament yesterday, everyone in town knew me, and people waved as we went by. *Of course* everyone knew Bindr, and his nephew was waiting on the steps of the library.

"Take this blank book, Uncle," he said, "and write to me."

"Aww," said Bindr, touched. "Keep your books and paper dry, nephew!"

We left for my home, feeling good...

We were prepared for villager *curse number one*: circling back. I wasn't sure whether I'd be affected or not, since Big Village wasn't *my* village. Bindr didn't think that he'd be affected himself, since he was a witch now, but we made sure to avoid taking any chances...

Jack tied us together with a long rope, and led the way into the mountains.

It was no problem! I actually started to circle back once, but with an easy tug on the rope from Jack, I was back in line.

"Interesting..." Bindr said, taking notes.

One curse down!

Curse number two—forgetting the village or what I was doing—was also solved with Jack's occasional, simple reminders: "Keep moving, we're rescuing Ru's parents..."

"Oh, right!" I exclaimed, marveling at how my mind was wiped and then suddenly remembered. "Onward!"

This time, I had company! This was an entirely different trip than before.

And *curse number three* of adopting a new village wouldn't be a problem for me— we were going to my home!

Now that the curses were out of the way, we just had to plod along, step by step. I knew that we would eventually pass by Smudge's Meadow, maybe camp at the *Spider Forest* camp, then either stop at Rabbit Valley or the camp where I first met Jack. From there, it would be a straight shot onto the plains, then home. *Home, sweet home!*

The day progressed. We began climbing the hills. "I wish we had horses!" Bindr grumbled. The weight of everything we were carrying seemed heavier with every step...

"Even one we could load stuff onto would be a huge help!" Jack added, shifting his backpack to his front for a while.

When we'd started walking at Big Village, I didn't even feel the weight of the golden apples. But now, after miles of trudging over the plains and heading into the hills, they felt like *nuggets of iron*.

"Golden Apples are heavy!" I exclaimed with a grunt.

"Well, it's too late to worry about it now," Jack said. "We'll just have to make do. Let's rotate our loads—it might make this easier." We did, swapping the apple load, potion load, and general provisions load. Smudge stayed with me.

To make things nicer, I made up another little song:

Home ... *clomp*...

Is ... *clomp*...

Getting ... *clomp*...

Close ... *clomp*...

With ... *clomp*...

Every ... *clomp*...

Step ... *clomp*...

We're taking ... *clomp*...

These potions ... *clomp*...

Golden Apples ... *clomp*...

We're friends ... *clomp*...

Soon zombies ... *clomp*...

we're unmaking! ... *clomp*...

The three of us joyously sang as we plodded along, our voices ringing in the hills. That night, we slept in the spider forest, using the existing camp, and sat with our backs to the log and a roaring fire in front of us.

Bindr, after a lifetime of reading, knew loads of funny stories, and the witch kept us entertained until bed. I chuckled at what the spiders must have thought of us— people roaring with laughter, long into the night? Whatever their thoughts, those arachnids thankfully stayed away...

I was a little worried about Smudge, wondering whether or not she'd remember her home. What would I do if she wanted to stay? If she'd leave us? *Well,* I thought. *You can't make a cat do anything.* So as my ocelot cuddled with me through the night, purring against my head, I hoped and hoped and hoped that she would choose *me*.

Rabbit Valley was still very full of rabbits.

When we arrived, it was too early in the day to make camp, but we decided to take a *meal break* in the shade of the rickety, old shelter. Besides—I wanted Smudge to be able look around. She did, chasing madly after rabbits, stalking them with her tail twitching. Smudge had a full belly, so didn't kill any, but many rabbits were terrified that afternoon...

I was packing up to go when I heard a 'merowt'. Smudge actually squeaked, and ran over to the corner of the shelter.

I saw other cats—two older ocelots, and three more that matched Smudge's age.

Her family...

Then, suddenly there were at least twenty cats all talking in their mysterious language!

It was heartwarming. Bindr watched with tears in his eyes—Jack too—and the tears were rolling unashamedly down my face, as I watched Smudge and thought that she's stay here for sure...

"I hope she doesn't want to stay," Jack cried. Who knew that everyone loved Smudge so much besides me?

"I'm sorry to interrupt," Bindr said, "but we need to go ... if we're going to make it to the first camp," sobbed Bindr. He was sobbing!

"I know!" I wailed. "Smudge, if you want to *stay*, we'll understand..."

My ocelot came over to me, rubbing against my leg. I picked her up and wiped my tears on her silky coat. I put her down and turned away to hide my anguish.

"We'll never forget you, Smudge." Jack said, blowing his nose on his shirt.

Bindr picked the cat up and squeezed her. "Bye, Smudge. We'll visit whenever we can! Have a good life..." The witch put her down and picked up his bag and walked quickly away.

I couldn't look back—I just started walking and didn't stop...

Goodbye, Smudge, I thought.

"Bye Smudge!" Jack said, then trotted to catch up to us.

"Meorwt!" Smudge exclaimed, running after us. Then, she climbed up my clothes to sit in her favorite spot on my chest, where she promptly fell asleep, no doubt wondering why people were so blazing mysterious and weird...

We spent another night on the road at the first camp, and the next day, we came out of the hills and into the plains. I couldn't see my village, but I *felt* it close. Maybe there was an *opposite side* of the curse...

It was great to be in my plains again, full of green grass and flowers! Some wild horse herds roamed tantalizingly out of reach...

"Still, it would be nice to have horses..." Bindr said.

Ah well, I thought. *If wishes were horses...*

Tiny sips of Bindr's healing potions kept us going strong, and it wasn't long before we reached Wolf Creek.

"Let's stop here for breakfast," Jack said. "It's such a nice little burbling stream. Then we can push on to Ru's home!"

"Sounds good to me," Bindr said.

"Come on, guys!" I replied with a smile. "I'll show you something cool that I have a story about! We're really close to home now, you know..."

The three of us put our things down and went a short way upstream to the flat rock where I had met the wolf before. I told them the story, and Jack thought that the idea of me hitting that wolf on the head with the *chicken leg* was hysterical! I did too, now it was over. We laughed and laughed.

Later, after splashing cold creek water on our faces and lounging for a while, we determined that it was time to go. I stood with the others and turned to head back down to the road, but I stopped dead in my tracks, too shocked to move...

"Ru," said Jack, grabbing my arm. "What's the matter?"

I pointed down at the road, and Jack looked and gasped. Then, he sprang into action!

"No!!" Jack yelled, running toward the herd of wild horses.

The animals had wandered over and found our stash of golden apples...

The horses were eating them!

"Gone!" Jack shouted angrily. "They're all gone!" The soldier was sitting next to the empty bag, holding his head and moaning. A horse nudged him with its face and nickered softly.

I still could not believe it. There was not *one apple* left...

Bindr kept shaking his head and clucking his tongue. Tsk tsk...

"But we were *ten feet away* from them!" I stammered. "How could we not *hear* them?!" I stomped up and down the road. A silver horse blocked my path, wanting to be petted. I glared up at it and the animal *burped* softly, smelling like apple...

"Unshod hooves on grass," said Bindr, "Tsk tsk."

"Who knew that horses could be so SNEAKY?!" yelled Jack, glaring at the buck with a black mane and tail.

"What do we do now?" I asked. I felt a sense of panic rising in me, and feared that my parents being saved was out of reach. And we were so close to home! "We can always get apples, but *gold?!* How do we get more gold?!"

I stomped and shook my head, then tried to calm myself down. Looking up, taking a deep breath, I reached out and patted the silver horse. He had nice eyes.

Was he sorry he had helped ruin our progress? I hoped so...

"Let me see your map," Bindr said suddenly. I pulled the map out of my pack and handed it to him.

The witch held it up and nodded, eyes moving quickly over the drawings, deeply contemplating...

"I have an idea." Bindr said finally. A pinto horse nudged the witch in the back, pushing him forward. "Stop it!" he snapped, then turned back to me. "There's an abandoned mine in the hills. There's usually a lot of gold left behind when a mine is closed. I think we should try and see if we can find some in there..."

407

I shook my head no. "But I need to get home!"

Bindr said, calmly, "Ru, we *need* golden apples. We cannot save your parents without them. It's only a day out of our way, and it's our best chance..."

Jack jumped and laughed as the buck next to him blew grass down his shirt. He patted the horse and spoke up, "I think we have horses now, at least. Maybe they'll let us ride them, or carry our things? That will cut the travel time down!"

"Horses *do* respond well to being given golden apples," Bindr said, patting the pinto that was bothering him.

Oh BLAZES.

Now we had horses, but no gold.

"Great..." I relied sarcastically.

"Shall we go and find more gold?" Jack asked with a grin.

"Sure," I said, patting the silver horse. "Let's head to the mines..."

Book 4

An Unofficial MINECRAFT Book

Gold in the Lost Mine

Ru, Jack, and Bindr (and Smudge the ocelot!) were on their way back to Ru's village to FINALLY cure his parents and the other villagers of the zombie curse when a herd of wild horses ate the golden apples they needed! Oh no!

Now their desperate idea to replace the lost gold leads the group to an abandoned mineshaft to search deep within the world. Will they find the gold they need to make more golden apples and save Ru's Mom and Dad? And can the novice warrior villager overcome whatever monsters lurk deep down in the Lost Mines?

Book 4, Chapter 1

We sat in the sunshine, looking at each other.

The only sounds were the normal noises of the plains: birds, wind, flapping of butterfly wings, and the sound of those blazing horses munching on grass!

Oh, blazes, those horses... I thought, frowning.

All of our hard work—our earnings from the tournament. Gone.

"We have a decision to make," Jack said. He was munching on a blade of grass himself. The buck with the black mane and tail was standing directly behind him, munching in the same rhythm. *Weird!*

The pinto was gazing near Bindr, occasionally raising her head to look at him. I could swear that she was smiling at the witch...

Smudge had her own horse too, it seemed. A cat with a horse? *Ridiculous!* But that's the way it appeared. Smudge the ocelot was curled on the back of a small black horse, and the nag was swishing her tail for Smudge to play with. The tail flicked to the left; Smudge reached out with her ocelot claws, stretching, a little more. Flick to the right. The cat overreached and slid off into the grass. Her horse nickered as if amused.

"Meowrt!" Smudge exclaimed, then jumped up lightly to start the game again.

I turned to see what the silver horse was doing. It seemed that it was this stallion who liked me most. I liked him too. He had a beautiful and shiny silver coat with a matching mane and tail. It was the color of gleaming armor. The steed's tail was long. He was big, and muscular, and looked like he could run forever.

But right now, he was ignoring me. Humph.

"Since these horses ate our golden apples," Jack said, "We're going to need more gold. The abandoned mine is the best place to find it, and sometimes there are golden apples left behind there too." Jack paused to look back at the black-maned horse when it shoved its face into his shoulder. "We can all go look for it, but I'm wondering if one of us should go on to the village..."

I nodded glumly. "I'll bet it's not going to be me."

"I should go," said Bindr. "I can get everything setup and I'll check on your parents too, Ru. I'll setup a brewing stand in case we need more potions."

"Sorry Ru," Jack said, avoiding looking at me. "Truth is, you're a great fighter, and we don't know what we'll run into down there." He knew how much I wanted to get back to my parents to make sure that they were okay. And by that, I meant that Mom and Dad were still *zombies*, locked in the basement waiting to be rescued, with my brother Brew watching over them and the house.

Just last week, if someone said I was a great fighter I would have laughed, but I guess after battling spiders, skeletons and bullies, and winning a real tournament, I should give myself a little credit.

Jack was right. I needed to lend my sword arm to the mission in the mine.

I groaned, and threw my head back. "You're right, Jack. Bindr, you head on to my village. Make sure my parents and Brew are okay, alright? Smudge should go with you too. Jack and I will get more gold and head home as soon as we can."

Jack and Bindr nodded.

"Sounds like the best way," the witch said.

I gave myself a moment to feel devastated that I wasn't going with home with Bindr and Smudge, then turned my thoughts to more cheerful matters.

"Hey," I exclaimed, "does anyone know how to ride a horse?"

There were a total of six horses in the herd, which was perfect. There was one for each of us, and two to carry things—*IF* the horses would agree to do it. We didn't have leads or saddles, so it was up to the horses to play nice and go where we wanted them to go.

I approached Silver cautiously, clicking my tongue and saying nice things like 'here boy' and 'what a pretty horsie!' He stared at me.

"Since you don't have a saddle," Jack called from nearby, "you have to grab his mane and leap on!" He was talking in a singsong voice, trying to convince his buck to let him up.

Bindr was somehow already on his pinto, and sat on its back, calmly watching us.

"How did you do that?" I asked. I tried to leap onto Sliver. The stallion sidestepped underneath me, and I ended up in a heap on the other side.

"Must be a witchy thing," Jack grumbled. He now had a rope on Bucky, but the horse was circling its hindquarters away from him, keeping its head nuzzling Jack's shoulder.

"Stand still!" the soldier commanded crossly, and to his surprise, Bucky immediately stopped.

Jack moved to his horse's side, grabbed the black mane with one hand and leapt up onto its back. "Hooray!" he shouted, and Bucky rolled his eyes.

Jack immediately slid off again—on purpose—then practiced getting on and off. He patted Bucky and gave him a carrot.

Crunch, crunch, crunch.

"I think we can use our *knees* to nudge them in the direction we want to go," Bindr said. "I read a book that said to press your knee into the side you want the horse to move away from, and it'll go the other direction."

"What?!" I asked. I hadn't even managed to sit on Silver yet.

"Hey, that works!" Jack exclaimed triumphantly, hands folded across his chest. He was nudging Bucky in circles and wavy patterns. Bucky was obliging with Jack's knees.

"See that?" I told Silver. "*That* is how we're supposed to do it."

Silver threw his head back and laughed at me.

In the end, sugar did the trick. "Ah ha!" I said, feeling the solid muscle and warmth under me. "I think I'm beginning to understand you, Silver. You help me, and I'll give you lumps of sugar. Deal?" My horse nodded and stamped at the ground.

I had a horse!

Silver was *my* horse!

We loaded up the two pack horses. They were good-natured, too. Bindr took one to the village, and Jack and I decided to take the other to help carry the gold back home—the gold I *hoped* we were going to find, anyway!

Before we split up, we all looked at the map.

From the first camp where we had stayed the night, instead of taking the shortcut to Rabbit Valley and then onto the Big Village, Jack and I would turn left, deeper into the extreme hills.

"Looks like there's deep ravine with a river that you'll have to cross," Bindr said, pointing at the map with a green tinged finger. "That could be tricky. Rivers run fast and deep in narrow places."

Gulp. I didn't like being near water in the first place. The thought of crossing deep, fast water made my stomach clench.

"Maybe we can circle around it." Jack said, frowning at the map. "It looks like there might be a way *here*." He pointed.

"What's that *squiggly line?*" I asked, squinting at the map. "It goes across the ravine."

"A bridge! It must be a bridge!" Jack replied excitedly.

"Great! Another problem solved," I said.

Maybe this wouldn't be too hard after all.

What was *hard* ... was getting the horses to understand that we were splitting up the herd. They wanted to stay together—so did we, really—but that wasn't going to happen.

Bindr took Smudge's horse and the one pack horse—a big white one—on rope leads. Jack and I similarly tied *our* pack horse—a small white one—on our own rope.

Then, we started off on in our separate directions.

Once the herd caught on to what was happening, the horses all suddenly stopped, refusing to move.

"Blazes!" I cried, looking around at our stubborn steeds, and at the other horses a short distance away with Bindr and Smudge.

Jack and I tried holding our horses while Bindr rode out of sight, but shortly after Bindr disappeared over the horizon, they all came trotting back! Bindr hung onto his Pinto's mane with a terrified expression on his face, and legs flying out behind. Smudge had her claws and teeth buried in Midnight's mane, standing on her hind legs so that she could see where they were going. The ocelot looked excited when her little black horse started to gallop. Her nose was pointed and green eyes slit against the wind, and cute ears laid down to keep the wind out.

"Any more ideas?" Bindr asked with a groan, standing by Pinto with his legs shaking.

"Blindfold them?" Jack suggested. "We used to do that to Sir Darwym's horses when they were being trained."

"Okay, let's try it." I said.

I looked at Silver. This was not going to be good.

Fifteen cubes of sugar later, and I had made zero progress. Silver refused to allow himself to be blindfolded, but definitely enjoyed the sugar! The other horses fared no better. They didn't get upset, or less

428

tame. They just all outright refused to separate.

"I give up!" said Jack. "This is taking more time than just going to the village."

I held my breath.

Bindr said, "I agree. We should all go to your home, Ru. Then we can pen the horses so you two can leave. Same plan; let's just go there first."

Yippee! My heart felt like it was going to burst out of my chest. I grinned. I still needed to go to the abandoned mine, but at least I'd know what was happening back home first!

With that, we all jumped onto our horses and galloped off toward home.

Home!

There were no problems, and Silver moved smoothly beneath me. "Thank you Silver," I whispered, and he twitched an ear back, as if to say 'you're welcome'.

I was headed home!

The village looked the same. We passed the rails where I had talked to Payj the librarian. *Was that only a week ago?* I wondered. *A little over a week?*

There it was! My house! Jack and Bindr held back a little as I galloped to the yard, and leapt off of silver to find my brother!

"Brew! Brew!" I shouted at the top of my voice.

Brew's head popped out of the shop door. He was smudged with soot, and gasped in surprise. "Ru! You're back!!" My brother ran to me, and gave me the biggest hug I ever had. "Oh, my Blazes! Oh my!" he kept saying over and over...

Eventually, he let me go. By that time, Jack and Bindr had ridden up dismounted and unloaded the horses behind me.

Brew looked totally confused. "You've got horses? You're wearing *armor?* Blazes! I can't wait to hear all about this!" Then he looked at the others and grinned. "Hi! I'm Ru's brother, Brew!" he said, going to help Jack lead Bucky to water.

We led the horses into the yard and shut the gate. "This is a place where you'll be safe, Silver, and there's lots of food!" My horse seemed to understand, because he immediately tromped over to mom's garden and started munching on her lettuce. I groaned. We'd have to fix that.

"Brew! How are Mom and Dad?" I asked, rushing up to my brother. I was afraid to know the answer, but it was time to find out.

"Fine," he said. "They're fine—still in the basement! They sleep during the day and try to get out at night, but they don't seem to be decaying or anything."

I sat down on a bench with a thud. "Thank the Blazes." I said softly. Smudge jumped off of Midnight (that's the name I gave her horse, since ocelots can't speak) and daintily walked over to me, then sat down, rubbing her face against my shoulder.

Brews' eyes popped out. "And you have a pet *ocelot* now? I can't wait to hear about this one! But first, do you have a cure? Can we change Mom and Dad back now?"

I shook my head. "We have part of the cure; a potion of weakness. We need golden apples. We *had* some—oh, I won the gold for em in a *tournament*, and you should have seen me, Brew! I was awesome! But then ... the horses ate them, which is why we have horses. We went to the nether to get blaze powder. And..."

"Wait, wait! I'm so confused!" Brew cried. "Come in and get some lunch. And you can fill me in!" If Brew was disappointed at the news, he didn't show it.

"Oh," I added. "And this is Bindr, Payj's friend, who was the librarian in Big

Village, but now he's a witch. He's in charge of potions and stuff."

"Hi! Thanks for your help!" Brew exclaimed, then walked us into the kitchen. He didn't even blink at the idea of a librarian turning into a witch.

I looked at the basement door, which Brew had reinforced with iron. He'd also put a little window in.

"It's so I can keep an eye on them," he said, seeing me look. I could hear the sadness in my brother's voice. It must have been awful to just wait and see if I even came back in one piece, let alone if I could even find and bring home a cure...

I gave Brew a fierce hug, biting back tears, then went to the basement door's little window. I couldn't see anything down there, but I said softly, "Mom, Dad, I'm doing it. Soon, you'll be back to normal. *I promise!*"

Book 4, Chapter 2

Leaving the village again was the hardest thing I'd ever done. And not because of the *triple villager's curse*, but because I realized how much I missed my family. Mom and Dad and Brew—I just wanted to stay near them.

But I did left anyway.

It had to be done.

We had filled my brother in on all of the details while eating freshly-roasted chicken and mushroom soup. Brew wanted to get the rest of the villagers together and have a big meeting, but I wanted to get going as soon as possible.

"The sooner we leave, the sooner we'll get back," I told him.

Brew didn't want me to go either. He was afraid that he'd never see me again. Heck—I was too!

Looking through the storefront's inventory, Brew and I scrapped together some armor for Jack to wear until we could make something decent. Brew said he'd start on Jack's armor right away while we were gone, and I knew that he'd make something special. After all, Jack was now part of the family.

While we ate, Brew filled us in on the zombie attacks. Apparently the men Sir Darwym left behind to patrol the town were actually *effective*. There had been no more attacks. *Weird*, I thought. It was almost like the zombies *knew* that the village was protected. Hmmmm...

Silver and Bucky had no problem leaving the herd behind this time. Maybe they knew that their family was safe at home. We obtained proper leads for the two horses, but I decided I that I still didn't want a saddle. Now that I was used to 'controlling' Silver with my knees, I didn't want to change anything.

I made sure to take a big bag of sugar with me on the mission to get more gold.

As a packhorse, we took the biggest of the white horses, who we named Blanco. He was the strongest steed, and gold is heavy! He was able to carry all our supplies easily enough—food and torches, empty bags and rope—while barely noticing the weight.

After camping at First Camp—as it was now and permanently called (by me) and labeled on the map—Jack and I took a left on a little trail up into the hills.

I was feeling pretty happy. The weight of not knowing whether or not my parents and Brew were okay was now gone;

440

lifted. And I was fairly confident that Jack and I could get through any challenges. We had already been through so much! Jack and I swapped tall takes, and sang a couple of tunes. It was fun.

Unlike the bigger paths through the mountains, this way was narrow, overgrown, and made the horses take their time, picking their way carefully through the dense terrain. Often times Silver, Bucky, and Blanco had to jump from one rock to another, but luckily the rocks were flat and not slippery.

Jack had picked up a nice black saddle for Bucky, to match his mane, and rode ahead, leading Blanco, while Silver and I followed up in the back. In the distance, we heard the constant roar of water.

We were approaching the ravine. It sounded like there was a waterfall. We stopped to rest the horses, and took a good look at the map.

"I don't see any falls on here, but I definitely hear them!" Jack said, studying the map doubtfully. "I hope this thing is accurate!"

"Me too," I added, not really looking at it. I figured that I'd worry with learning how to read the map once we made it to the mine.

Finding the way across didn't take long. We walked around one big rock and there was a ravine—deep and twisted with a loud, rushing river running through it. There were falls on the right, and a nice little bridge going across not too far from us.

"Ah, this looks easy!" Jack exclaimed cheerfully.

"Uhhhh..." I stammered.

Yikes! I thought. I didn't think so. It was a long way down. What if the bridge snapped under our weight? What if I slipped?!

"Oh, come on," Jack said, slipping off of Bucky and leading his horse forward. The pair went across the bridge with no problem, Bucky's hooves *clomping* on the wooded slats.

"Okay Blanco," I said, waving at Jack. "Go over to the carrot."

Jack produced and waved around a bright orange carrot. Blanco took notice, and passed over over the bridge easily—at least partway.

Blanco was a big heavy horse, and was loaded with supplies. When he made it halfway across the ravine, we heard a huge *creak*...

"Run, Blanco!" I yelled.

The big white packhorse didn't need any urging. At the first shift of the boards under his massive hooves, the stallion took off for the opposite side. He made it, but ... the bridge didn't. The creaky wooden structure snapped and broke apart in the middle, leaving Silver and I stranded on the wrong side!

I stared across the ravine.

Jack stared helplessly back.

"You'll have to go around, Ru!" he yelled over the sound of the falls.

Oh Blazes, I wished I had taken a closer look at the map! "Okay!" I shouted back.

Silver stamped at the ground anxiously, but didn't give me any problems when I signaled for him to turn off to the right. I figured that we'd follow the cliffs upstream until we could find another way across, then head back to the path to find Jack.

Jack paced along with us on the other side. When Silver and I passed the falls, the river widened out, and slowed down.

Finding a way across looked promising.

Holy Blazes, I thought, catching sight of something helpful up ahead. There was a higher road! The path led to a nice little *landing pier* jutting out over the water, and there was a little boat. Across the river was a matching pier and a little shelter.

It was the perfect place to spend the night!

Now ... I just had to get the boat across. Problem was, I'd never been in a boat before...

There wasn't room for Silver in the boat. "Silver, I hope you can swim," I told him. He put both hooves in the water, and looked at me evenly. He seemed ready.

"How about you get Silver over, then I'll follow in the boat!" I yelled to Jack across the way.

"Okay," he yelled back. "*Come on Silver!*"

Silver looked at me, then decided to go across. The river became deeper in the middle, but my horse navigated without a problem.

It was my turn.

I shakily climbed into the boat, untied it from its mooring on the shore, and pushed off. The old, wooden boat glided smoothly across the surface of the river, then started to drift...

Before long, I found myself floating downstream...

"You've got to *row!*" screamed Jack. "Use those sticks—they're *oars!* See em? Use em!"

"Oh. Okay," I replied—too softly for Jack to hear—then I grabbed the oars and started using them to row the boat across the water. The current caught me and started to push me downstream towards the waterfall...

I suddenly realized: *waterfall*.

Oh, Blazes!

"Row, Ru!" Jack screamed, waving his arms frantically. I could see the frightened whites of his eyes from far away.

I dug into the water with the ends of the oars and rowed with all my might. For a while, I felt myself still drifting toward the roaring waterfall, and for a while thought that I wasn't moving at all! But then, I finally began to make a little headway. Row by row, inch by inch against the current, I eventually made it to the other side. Jack and the horses waited for me to walk the boat back up to its dock on *this* side of the river.

"You know," Jack said afterwards, "You should have started rowing right away." He watched me tie the boat onto the mooring.

"I know that NOW," I said panting. Rowing is hard work! "A lot of help *you* were, Silver," I groaned.

Silver shook his head and stamped at the ground. I think he was laughing at me!

Jack and I checked the map. "I think we're in luck," said Jack. "This high road here looks like it leads right to the abandoned mine. Good work, Ru!"

But the road wasn't on the map.

"I wonder what *else* isn't on the map?" I said. But there was no time to worry about it. It was getting dark. We had to set up camp and get some good rest for the morning.

I woke early to Silver snorting at me.

Once Jack was up too, we were both anxious to get to the abandoned mine and check it out. After we packed everything up and hit the road while the morning was still pale and quiet, our path led us straight to the mine.

The place was old, and run down, and had obviously been abandoned for a long time.

Near the sagging entrance was an old corral, so Jack and I put the horses into it and prepared many torched. We would definitely need them.

"Are you going to be okay here, Silver?" I asked, patting my stallion and giving him a sugar cube. "You've got water and grass and ... there's a little overhang for shade. We should be back soon." I looked away from my horse at my soldier companion. "Jack, are they gonna be okay if we just leave them here?"

Jack looked around. We were far into the wilderness. This place was truly abandoned. "I think they'll be okay. I hope so."

"What if we don't come back?"

"Bucky," Jack said, looking at his black-maned horse, "If we don't come back, you go home, alright?"

Bucky rested his head on Jack's shoulder.

"And you get help, Silver, if we don't come back," I said to my horse. "Blanco, you stay with your brothers." Blanco was a sweet horse. I was worried about them, but not *totally* worried. They were wild horses after all, and had taken care of themselves for years before eating our *blazing* golden apples...

Jack and I turned to face the dark, dusty entrance to our new, dangerous adventure.

It was time for the mine.

I'd never been in one before. Unlike a cave, this place was definitely manmade—carved into the mountain and shored up with wooden beams—and the floors were smooth and well-traveled.

We stepped inside, each holding a torch and a sword.

There were old torches left on the walls from ages past, so we lit them as we passed. We wouldn't be getting lost in here, *no-siree!* Cutting across the tunnels were creaky, rusty rails and old, shoddy mine carts. I was really happy to see that the tunnels at least were well built. Thick, old wooden beams held up the walls and ceilings, making sure that there'd be no cave-ins.

"Should we ride some carts and see where they go?" I asked.

"I don't think so," Jack said. "What if the tracks are broken, ending in mid-air?"

Sensible point, I thought.

So we walked. And walked. Our footsteps echoed, and we walked some more.

"Oh, there's a chest!" I announced suddenly, sighting an old, dusty wooden container. I ran over to it and opened the lid to peer inside...

Nothing.

"Here's another one." Jack said, rushing to a chest that was left sitting in an old mine cart. "Gah—also empty..."

We walked on for hours it seemed, checking each dark and dusty corridor that we passed. The entire place had been cleaned out!

Now what?

We Jack and I made the journey back towards the main entrance, disappointed and peering around, hoping to see something we'd missed, I extinguished the torches on the walls as we went. We were both way too discouraged to even talk, but Jack managed to speak up.

"We'll find a way Ru, don't you worry."

Honestly, I wasn't very sure that this was going to work. We did all that work, and it was for nothing.

"Too bad golden apples don't grow on trees," I muttered.

At least we didn't get lost.

When we finally caught sight of the exit, seeing the light of day pouring down from the shored-up mine entrance, and I heard a voice. Someone was there! We ran outside to the corral, swords drawn. No one was going to mess with our horses!

A man was standing there, petting Blanco. Silver and Bucky were eating a nice bucketful of carrots.

"Why, hello there!" The man exclaimed, turning to greet us. He had long hair and a huge bushy beard.

"Hello," said Jack wryly, cautiously lowering his sword. I left my drawn, just in case.

"I'm Ralph! You boys havin fun explorin the mine?"

The man's beard was so big that I couldn't even see his mouth move when he talked. Ralph seemed harmless. The horses seemed to like him, so maybe he was okay...

"Yeah sure," I replied, sheathing my sword. "I'm Ru, and this is Jack, Blanco, Silver, and Bucky. Do you live around here, Ralph?"

"Sure do, Ru! Hey—that rhymes!" He cackled, and Jack and I exchanged glances. "I don't get much company up 'round here, just people wantin to have fun in the mine."

"What are you *doing* up here?" Jack asked curiously.

"Well, I just like *building*. I've got a little house I'm working on near here." Ralph said. "I get some interesting rocks from the mine sometimes and add them to my place. Wanna see?"

I looked at Jack and shrugged. *May as well*, I thought. Maybe Ralph had some gold that we'd be able to trade for, since the mine was empty. "Sure, we'd love to!"

"Your horses'll be safe here. My house is just around the back!" Ralph led the way up a little footpath and we saw his place.

It was huge.

I mean—hos house was bigger than my village! There were windows and doors all over! The mansion was decorated with all kinds of rocks I'd never seen before: black, blue, even green. Sadly, I saw no gold...

My jaw dropped open looking over the massive structure.

"Whoa..." Jack breathed next to me.

"Come in, come in!" Ralph exclaimed, waving his hands as he scampered up to the front.

He led us inside, and Jack and I looked around in awe.

I figured that Ralph was happy to have visitors. This place must have been so much work to build! Some of the areas of the structure didn't make sense, but there were parts I really liked.

"It's amazing," I saw quietly, gazing around.

"Let me get you some food," Ralph said with a smile that moved his beard and moustache. "I've got a fabulous garden!"

The old man led us to a dining hall, and disappeared to prepare a dinner. The dining room was huge, with a giant wooden table. Before long, I started feeling restless. I needed to find some gold to save my parents, and while it was nice to see Ralph's place, this wasn't solving our problem...

Ralph eventually returned and served us some roast pork, bread, and some nice greens.

"Thank you," we said.

"So what were you all doin down there? Just explorin?" the old man asked while we ate.

I decided that it wouldn't hurt to tell him a little about our adventure. "We were looking for gold," I said.

Ralph laughed. "That mine doesn't have a stick left in it! I know—I scoured every inch. Lots of people come up here lookin for gold, and all the loot was taken out of it long ago. Whaddaya want *gold* for?"

"I need either gold or golden apples to save my parents from being zombies."

Ralph stopped laughing and became serious. "Oh ... I'm sorry, kid. That's tough. Tell you what," he said, thumping his fist on the table. "You've been real *kind* to an old hermit, and you have a just cause." I held my breath. Did he have a sack of gold we could take? "That map you've got there— that's just a map I made years ago, just to mess with people. But I've got the *real* one. I'll let ya have it..."

The old man walked over to a bookcase and pulled out a scroll of paper. He unrolled it onto the dining table, pushing plates out of the way. Some of the map's features were the same, but this one included the high road, waterfall, and Ralph's house. Some features were also a little different...

"Here. Right here," he said, pointing to a spot on the map not far from his house. "*This* is the entrance to the mine you want—the *real deal*. It's loaded with gold, gems and danger."

Jack and I exchanged glances, grinning. Could it be? Did we still have a change?

"Perfect!" I exclaimed with a smile.

Book 4, Chapter 3

Jack stared at Ralph. "A fake map? Really?"

Why would the old man distribute fake maps to the people of the area? Maybe he wanted to keep people away from the real mine by having them find the empty mine instead, returning home empty-handed...

Ralph looked a little ashamed. At least I think he did. It was hard to tell underneath all of that facial hair. But the old man did look down at his feet and hem and haw a little.

"Yeah, I know," he replied, looking up at us again. "But I was getting too many people *visitin*—which wasn't bad, but they'd wanna spend the night in my nice, comfy house instead of sleeping outdoors. Folks started havin *big parties* in my yard, and eatin up all my veggies. They started lootin the mine..." Ralph looked away wistfully, then back to us. His eyes were really big; *sad* even. "I just ... started bein terrified in my own house. They were botherin me all the time. I couldn't breathe..." Poor guy. It must have been terrible for a man who's a recluse to live in party central. "So I spread a little *false information*. I made sure the empty mine was *totally* cleaned out." He shrugged.

470

"After a while, when adventurers started coming back out of it with nothin, people stopped coming around."

"I understand," Jack said. "I'd do the same thing."

"Yeah," I added. "Sounds like you came up with a good resolution for your problem."

The old man smiled, and seemed relieved. "Thank you, boys."

"Now what do you know about the real mine?" Jack asked.

"Not much," Ralph replied. "It was abandoned a long time ago, along with the road. I went in, but not too far, because it's *real spooky*." He shivered. "I meant it when I said there was *danger* in there."

I looked at Jack. Jack looked at me, then turned back to Ralph. "You don't happen to have a chest of gold lying around, do you?" the soldier asked with a chuckle.

Ralph shook his head and replied simply, "Gold isn't of any use to me. It's too *soft*. Any gold I found, I just threw back into the deep mine shafts." He turned to me. "I'm sorry, kid."

I didn't doubt his sincerity, but *he threw it away?!* I was horrified!

"Blazes," I muttered. "That's too bad."

Ralph stared longingly in the distance as we silently sat for a moment. Then he shook his head and stood. "You two should stay the night," he said. "Get some rest. I'll look after the horses for ya."

I looked at Jack questioningly. *Should we do it?* I thought.

The soldier seemed to read my mind.

"Let's do it," Jack said. "If there's gold in this *Lost Mine*—" He glanced at Ralph, who nodded until his beard flopped over his head, "...It's our best bet I guess."

After that long, long day of walking through a useless mine and dealing with disappointment, I was ready to sleep. First though, I hiked back down to Silver and told him what happened. My horse listened, or maybe he was snoozing. It was hard to tell.

The next morning, I woke up bright and early, ready for gold and danger. After fresh coffee and bread, then a quick chat with Silver, I was ready to go.

Ralph handed Jack and me a bag of rocks. "I thought about it last night," the old man said, "and these here might help ya..."

I opened the bag, and inside were some glowing pebbles.

"What are these?"

"Glowstone," Ralph replied. "Leave em to mark your path so ya don't get lost in there. Maybe this'll help you kids."

I was touched. "Thanks, Ralph. And thanks for talking care of the horses."

Jack took the fake map and borrowed a quill, making a big X on it. "This is Ru's village," he said. "Ralph, will you go for help if we don't come back?"

Oh Blazes, this was way too serious. "Of course, we'll come back, Jack!" I exclaimed. "But it's always good to be prepared, right?"

Jack replied without hesitation. "Of course, Ru. We'll be fine. But will you, Ralph?"

"Sure I will, kid."

We gathered our supplies, torches, food and rope. It was time to go mining.

Wow, there was *such* a difference between the empty mine and this other one. Where the first mine was kind of bright and airy, this one was dank and stale, like no air had circulated though the deep, pitch-black tunnels in a long time. There weren't any nice torches on the wall waiting to be lit either...

"I'll be glad when we're done with this place," Jack said, tying his shirt over his nose. His voice echoed through the corridors. "This stinks."

"Worse than Smelly," I laughed. *Good idea*, I thought, then I tied my short over my face too. Breathing was suddenly much better.

The tunnels were old with dusty cobwebs in the corners, and there were many areas missing beams in the supports. I found myself worrying about cave-ins almost constantly.

We found one chest right away, but it was empty.

"I think we'll find a lot of gold here," Jack said. "I just have that feeling."

"I hope so." I was sure that we would find something—either gold, or something, creepy, crawly, or disgusting...

Jack and I marked our way through the dark corridors with the glowstone pebbles, putting them in certain places so that we'd know which tunnel to take going back. The place was very confusing—everything crisscrossed—and there were many dead ends where the tunnel had collapsed, or where excavation had simply stopped.

At first, I tried to make a note of which way were were going. Left, right, right, left, then back again, then right. But my mental notes became twisted, and I lost it all. Too confusing.

Eventually, I had a horrible realization.

"Jack, I don't know which way to go." I said quietly, staring at the corridors leading away from a dark intersection. They were all the same.

"That's easy," Jack said, "we go back *this* way." He turned around. There was no glowstone in sight. Everything looked the exactly the same. "Oh no," he said. "We're lost!"

I gasped, and felt a cold dread building up in my stomach.

We were lost in the *Lost Mine*...

"Don't panic," I exclaimed, panicking. "I'm sure we can find our way out..."

My heartbeat was suddenly a lot faster.

"Right," Jack said, swallowing heavily. "We just need to *think*. Think, think, think..."

I took a deep breath and let it out slowly.

"Okay," I said. "So we have glowstone leading us out. We've been dropping it, right?"

"Right." Jack closed his eyes. He squeezed them shut.

"So ... we just need to find the last one that we dropped. It can't be far."

Jack opened his eyes, and started looking around. "We have three possible tunnels. What if *one of us* stays here, and the other tries each tunnel until we find glowstone?"

"Yes. YES!" I exclaimed, nodding, looking at the thick stone walls all around us. The stone went on for a long way on the other side of the wall. We were so deep in the ground. I was too restless to stand in one place. "You stay here—I'll look."

I started off in one direction, feeling very small and lost.

"Wait!" Jack said suddenly, grabbing my arm. "Tie a rope around your waist, just in case, Ru!" Jack handed me the rope, and tied the other end to *his* waist.

"Just in case," I repeated solemnly.

I took a torch, and headed down the first tunnel. The corridor didn't go far before ending in a dead end.

"Not this way..." I said to myself, peering at the thick cobwebs in the corners.

I retraced my steps, coiling the rope back up in one hand as I went. Collecting the rope wasn't as easy as I expected with one hand, but there was *no way* I was putting down my torch...

I made it back to Jack and shook my head.

"Any glowstone?" he asked.

"Dead end," I replied.

Jack stepped forward and put a random piece of wood across it the tunnel's entrance.

"Wouldn't it be funny if they were *all* dead ends?" Jack asked, trying to crack a smile. "Spooky!" But his humor immediately backfired. What if? I felt fear reach up in me, and Jack's face seemed to pale as well.

I continued exploring, and the second tunnel had a sharp bend in it. Another dead end perhaps? I turned the corner, nearly at the end of my rope...

And saw two chests!

"Yippee!" I hooted, which echoed through the tunnel.

"What?" Jack's voice echoed back from far behind me.

"Chests!" I shouted. "Hang on!"

"What?" Jack shouted back.

"Chests!"

"A nest?!" Jack shouted back, his voice echoing. "A nest of cave spiders? Come back!!"

"No ... *chests!*"

I shook my head, planted my torch, then flung open the lid of the first container. Inside was a nice bunch of emeralds and some seeds. "Cool!" I said to myself, gathering it all up. Then I went to the second chest.

Taking a deep breath, I slowly opened the lid, hoping for the best.

The pale yellow gleam reflecting my torchlight from inside was like roast chicken for the soul.

Gold.

I smiled, suddenly terrified that we'd never make it back to save Mom and Dad.

Picking up some gold with trembling hands, I held it for a moment, then carefully placed all of the gold into a bag. I remembered to look around, just in case there was another chest, but this was it. Retrieving my torch, I followed the rope back to Jack.

"Jack! Look!" I exclaimed. He had been waiting with a severely worried face.

I opened my heavy bag and showed him the gold, and the relief on his face was huge.

"Gold!" he exclaimed with a smile.

"Is it enough?" I asked, hopeful.

"No, but it's a good start, and we know we're on the right path." Jack handed the bag back to me and I tucked it away.

"Let's make sure that we can find out way out," I said, "then come back to here. Maybe there's more chests further down. I didn't have enough rope to check."

Jack nodded. "Good idea." He placed another board onto the rocky floor pointing towards the promising tunnel.

Just to be sure, I continued our plan and went down the third tunnel alone.

I saw the faint light of the glowstone up ahead on the ground.

Yes! I thought with a grin, and went back to Jack.

"That must be it, huh?" he asked when I appeared.

"Yeah. It's the way out. Should we go to the entrance now or go further in?"

"I was really scared that we were lost," the soldier said, staring at the darkness of a tunnel. "I'd feel better if we made our way out first, then came back. You know—just to be sure..."

He was scared. Clearly.

Come to think of it, I'd never seen Jack so afraid.

The two of us made our way back to the mine's entrance, making sure that we could see our glowstone path clearly coming and going.

Stepping outside into the sunshine, it felt good get some fresh air for a minute. The bright noon sun hurt my eyes.

"Feels like we've been in there for days," I said, looking back at the dark entrance. "Are you sure we don't have enough gold now?"

Jack shook his head. "Believe me, I wish it was enough." He took a deep breath. "Ready for more?"

"Yep!" I stood and took one giant lungful of mountain air, savoring its sweetness.

We delved into the darkness again, eventually making our way back down to the tunnel with the two chests. It was amazing how close those chests actually were, heading straight there without exploring every branch along the way.

Further down along an old, stale corridor with creaky mine tracks on the floor was another chest. Inside was more gold! *Yay!* Jack and I did a little dance, then

Jack put the gold into his bag. We were on a roll.

We carefully placed glowstone in strategic areas, and made sure that we could see it as we traveled along. Finding just a little more gold would do it, and we could get out of there!

Jack and I were eventually laughing and talking when turned around a bend and things changed. Very suddenly, the tunnel we were in *sloped down* at an unexpectedly steep grade, and both of us slipped and slid down into darkness!

"Catch the wall, Ru!" Jack cried as we rushed down into the unknown depths. He wasn't catching the wall himself.

"I'm trying!" I shouted. And I was, but we were sliding too fast, and I couldn't catch hold of anything!

We slid faster and faster, then fell through pitch-black open air—my heart leapt!—until *SPLASH!* We ended up in the middle of an underground lake...

As soon as I hit the water, I started splashing madly.

I didn't know how to swim. I broke the surface and thrashed my arms again, and managed to stay up, even though the weight of my armor tried to pull me down. It was a good thing I was so strong...

"Jack! Jack!" I half screamed, half sputtered. I couldn't see my friend. I was lost in the utter darkness, struggling in black waters...

Jack popped up next to me, gasping for breath. When he noticed me, thrashing around himself, he choked out, "Ru! Are you okay?"

"I don't know how to swim! Help!!"

I kept moving my arms and legs, anything to keep afloat.

"You ARE swimming, Ru! Keep doing what you're doing!" Jack started keeping his head above water, then seemed to calm down. He looked around, no doubt seeing just as little as I was. It was *really* dark. Our torches had been snuffed out by the water.

"But I don't ... I can't ... I'm too heavy ... I ... uh ... *oh*." I said, calming down. I found that moving my legs and arms in a certain pattern kept me afloat.

"Now that you can swim," Jack said, splashing as he treaded water. "I think we have another problem."

Oh Blazes. "What?"

"We're in a current," he said. "I think we're moving."

Great! I thought, frowning in the darkness. We were caught in the current of an underground river, barely able to swim.

What's next?! I thought crossly. I wasn't moving fast, but I could feel the river carrying us along...

"We need to look for a way out." Jack said. "Look ahead and see if you see a place we can climb out of the water."

I kept my eyes focused forward. Fortunately, the cavern wasn't entirely dark. Pockets of lava came and went. We could see some here and there by the orange glow. I was suddenly very glad we didn't land IN lava...

After a while, though, I was getting tired. My armor was heavy, and the gold in my bag was heavier. But there was no way I was going to ditch either. Or so I hoped.

"Keep your lungs half-full," Jack said. "You can float better."

I tried my friend's suggestion, and it helped a lot.

Eventually, floating along in the dark, I noticed the air seeming brighter—a little fresher, even...

"Jack!" I whispered.

"I see it, Ru," he whispered back.

We were floating into a giant cavern. There was more light up ahead, and I sighted a rocky ledge where we could hopefully grab on and pull ourselves out of the water.

The place was eerie. The light was a soft glowing blue.

I couldn't quite place it, but I had the feeling that some huge, ancient creature was roaming around in the darkness...

"There," I whispered. "Let's get out there!"

"Quiet," Jack breathed. He felt it the presence too.

But we had to get out of the water. The river could take us anywhere, perhaps keep us underground forever, or sweep us out to sea—maybe even over a waterfall! And I was getting more and more exhausted by the second...

Keeping my arms underwater, I paddled my way toward the rocky ledge dipping down into the black river.

We gradually approached the edge of the water, and suddenly the current became weaker. I was surprised to find my feet touch solid stone underwater, and pretty soon, I could stand. I didn't see anything around me, but I felt something ... or someone ... nearby.

Jack slowly followed me to the rocky shore, then climbed out of the water, trying not to make a sound. He was trying to be stealthy, so I did too.

I snuck out of the water, trying not to even drip.

At least we could see where we were now. The two of us gazed around a giant cavern full of all kinds of armor, books, and bottles; stuff scattered all over the cave floor, which was lined with luxurious *carpet!* The items were all covered in dust, but I could feel their power radiating at me.

"An enchanted cavern," Jack said softly, his voice filled with awe.

Book 4, Chapter 4

Much to my relief, it seemed that nobody was home. The feeling I'd experienced of a heavy *presence* around us was apparently the energy itself—the life of enchanted items.

"There's no telling how long it's been since anyone's been here," Jack said, looking around. His voice echoed strangely.

"Wow," I breathed, overwhelmed with awe and majesty. Was this place enchanted by the same person who'd built the high road and the ancient mine? This cavern was magical. "Oh, look!"

We approached a huge, stone platform that stood out from its carpeted surroundings. It was carved from bare stone. On top of the big platform were three strange, black tables with big, thick books closed and resting on top of each.

"Three enchantment tables," Jack said.

I didn't know anything about *enchantment*, but this place was cool! Two of what Jack called *enchantment tables* faced each other, while the third faced the shore and the water. Each table was surrounded by a ring of low bookshelves, were filled with glowing books...

Behind the bookcases were neatly stacked areas full of different items: armor, weapons, potions, and more! There were chests, too—lots and lots of chests—lining the walls of the cave between the various sections.

Two tunnels led into the enchanted cavern: one to the right, the direction from which we'd come, and one to the left, following the path of the river's current. Hopefully one of those tunnels would lead us up and out.

Jack cautiously walked up to one of the enchanting tables, being careful not to touch it. I looked at it more closely, following behind him. I didn't know what weird black stone the thing was made out of, but its top corners were green, and the book sitting on top, coated in dust, suddenly floated up into the air as Jack approached, rotating slowly.

"Blazes..." I said.

As Jack approached, the big book opened and spun toward him. Magical letters and symbols that I didn't recognize materialized as if made from light, and floated around the soldier's head...

Transfixed, Jack looked at the book, then backed away slowly, as if he didn't want to startle it.

"Anderwyn..." I said out loud, reading an inscription carved into the stone.

The word appeared and hung in the air.

Creepy.

Jack turned to me. "I think we should go."

"Okay," I said. "Let's just check the chests for gold, and not touch anything else." I started for the area full of containers...

"I don't think you should touch anything, Ru. We'll find ... *another* way to get gold." Jack kept looking over his shoulders, nervous as heck, first one way and then the other.

"What? Do you hear something?" I asked, feeling my friend's uneasiness.

Jack turned toward me and looked back at the tunnel; the place where we came in, floating in the river. He started to open his mouth, and an arrow suddenly *whizzed* by my head, narrowly missing me! We were under attack!

"Skeletons!" Jack shouted, pulling his sword and crouching in reflex.

Immediately, I grabbed a chest, spun it around to face the skeletons—I could see several climbing up from the water, their bones *clunking*, training their bows on us—and I flung open the lid, protecting our lower bodies with a little bit of improvised cover. Jack pulled a shield off of the wall, and raised it to protect both of us. We had moved like one smooth fighting machine...

The chest was filled with gold. Naturally, I grabbed as much as I could, stuffing my bag. Then I put more into Jack's. One way or another, we were going to get out of there *with gold*. There was also a bag of diamonds inside the chest, so I grabbed that too. If somehow we didn't have enough gold, I figured in the moment that we could use diamonds to trade for more gold.

Now we just had to escape alive...

I peeked through the hinge gap of the chest. Skeletons were pouring out of the river! I could imagine those bones walking along the black river's bottom, reaching at us with their skeletal claws as we floated by above, none the wiser. A shiver ran down my spine.

Then I noticed a huge rock hanging over the river's entrance. If only we could knock it down and block the tunnel; it would slow down the river, but also cut off more skeletons from coming in. Then, hopefully, we could deal with the skeletons stuck in the cavern at least...

"Jack, the rock!" I hissed. He looked, and immediately caught on to my idea.

"Cover me," he shouted, grabbing a bow and bunch of arrows from a stack of weapons behind us. The arrows glowed. I hoped that whatever magic was imbued into the missiles would give Jack an edge against skeletons, or breaking rocks!

The soldier stood and started shooting. He pelted the huge rock above the river, and I saw the arrows explode and pierce through the stone! *Oh*, I thought. *Maximum damage to rocks*. I grabbed a shield and fended off skeleton's incoming arrows, struggling to protect Jack.

I even managed to throw a horseshoe or two, taking out skeletons with a clang and a rattle! BAM! It felt good to score a direct hit and see an undead archer explode into loose bones.

Jack shot again and again at the weakest point of the boulder's connection to the cavern wall. Finally, it cracked, then burst, and the weight of the gigantic stone pulled it down, making a tremendous splash and mostly sealing the tunnel with a great, wet crash!

I half expected the whole cavern roof to come down, but either it was really strong or magically enchanted. It didn't budge. Yay! We lived!

Now, we just had to deal with thirty or so skeletons that hissed and growled and clambered toward us, firing their bows. *Great*. At least there weren't hundreds. I hoped that the falling boulder would have crushed some of them. Of the ones underwater when the rock came splashing down, who knows? Now, most of the advancing skeletons were a short distance away. They fired upon us with glowing bows.

"Ru, the bows are enchanted!" Jack hollered, shooting his own.

"I can see that!"

The shields we were using seemed to be enchanted as well, so maybe they canceled each other out. Whatever magic the skeletons' bows had didn't do them much good—their arrows bounced harmlessly off of our shields.

But then some of the skeletons started circling around, trying to get to us from the side.

Blazes!

I swiveled our chest-cover to give us more shelter, then grabbed another shield with my other hand. Jack and I were protected like a little, shelled creature.

But it wouldn't last. Already, a couple of the nearest skeletons had put their bows away, and drawn swords...

512

"They'll get us into a sword fight, and the others will pick us off!" Jack said grimly over the noise of arrows bouncing off of our shield wall. "And I'm running out of arrows! We need to do something else."

I looked around. There wasn't a lot in reach. But I had an idea.

"Jack, can you scoot backward?"

"Sure." He shuffled backward, while I dragged the chest and held up my shields. We only needed to move a little ... just a little farther...

There! I thought with a grin. We backed into a shelf full of axes, all glowing.

I picked one axe up and threw it at the nearest cluster of skeletons, ducking down quickly out of the way of their returning arrows. BAM! The enchanted axe crashed through two skeletons in one blow!

"Sweet!" I shouted. I love enchantments!

Jack picked up another quiver of arrows from a nearby shelf, immediately rushing back to the safety of my shield wall. He began aiming for the skellies who were trying to sneak up on the sides to flank us.

Jack's speedy arrows knocked the skeletons backwards, breaking their bones.

As long as we didn't run out of weapons, we'd be fine!

That is, until the *cave spiders* joined in...

Small arachnids appeared from nowhere with the chittering of fangs and rustling of their bristly legs. They came crawling down the walls out of unknown crevices in the cavern ceiling...

"Spiiiiidders!" Jack screamed, shooting them as fast as he could.

He ran out of arrows again.

I looked around frantically. "There, on that wall! A *diamond sword!*"

Jack dashed over, hiding behind his shield as he ran, grabbed the gleaming blue blade, and started slicing the spiders into nasty pieces. The fantastic sword cut through them like butter! "It must have some kind of *anti-spider spell!*" he shouted gleefully. "Take that!!" *Swipe*. "And That!" *Swipe, swipe*...

Soon, spider legs were raining down on my head. Yuck. I kept throwing axes at the small army of skeletons and protecting us with my shields.

Stretching to quickly look down at the advancing undead, I laughed. We were almost out of skeletons!

Then there was a loud splash.

516

I looked back to the river, and saw that the fallen boulder blocking the tunnel was moving. There were bony, little fingers poking out around its edges!

"Jack!" I cried. "The skeletons are moving the rock! We've gotta get out of here!"

"Alright—let's go, Ru! Grab whatever you can!" he yelled back.

We grabbed a bunch of stuff off the shelves—I scrounged up whatever I could get my hands on after dropping the extra shield—throwing it on top of the gold and diamonds, then turned and ran to the far tunnel, holding the shields behind us...

A couple of arrows plinked off of my shield as we ran down a nice wide tunnel. Neither Jack nor I were hit.

We ran like all blazes were after us...

And it was a good idea. Once that rock was moved, there was no doubt a huge army of skeletons coming after Jack and me!

"They must be there to protect the cavern," Jack panted as we hurried down the dark tunnel.

While there wasn't any light from torches—and neither of us stopped to light a torch—there were at least pockets of lava pools one side of the path, so I could see just fine. The weapons we'd taken glowed, too.

Finally, after running for a long time, I stopped and looked back. Jack stopped, looking back at me.

We weren't being followed.

"Blazes! We got away!" Looking around, I saw a nice rock was on the side of the tunnel. I was tired! "I'm gonna sit for just a minute—"

"Wait!" said Jack, "We don't know if there are any traps!"

But it was too late.

I sat down, unable to stop myself, and the block weirdly *dissolved* beneath me, leaving me falling into a swarm of bugs!

"Aaaaaugh!!" I screamed as they swarmed all over me. Tiny, nasty creatures were pinching and biting any part of my skin that they could reach!

"Ru!" Jack's hand poked through the twisting mass of biting insects and hauled me up out of the pit. Little silver bugs dropped off, their legs trying to get a grip on my armor. So many legs!

I sprinted away, shaking and shuddering, skin crawling, and turned to look back. *Thousands* of them were pouring out of the block I had broken! Their shiny little backs were reddish-silver in the light of the bubbling magma, and the swarm of them looked like a rippling carpet squirming toward us...

A couple of faster bugs reached us ahead of the mass of them, and Jack swept his enchanted sword through them, close to the ground.

"Let's just get out of here!" I shouted. "I won't touch anything else!"

Next to bats, bugs creeped me out the most, and who knew what other nasty surprises were waiting down here...

Luckily, Jack and I were on the right side of the bug swarm trap to make it out.

We continuing down the tunnel in a quick jog, then eventually slowed down to a walk.

Up ahead was a constant roar of rushing water.

"Does that sound like a waterfall to you?" I asked Jack. It looked like perhaps daylight lied ahead as well...

The way out? I wondered with a broad smile. I sighed and started heading toward—

"I think so. Wait—STOP!" Jack shouted, grabbing my arm.

"What?!"

"Tripwires! Look!"

I froze, and peered ahead, squinting...

It was a good thing that we were heading out instead of heading in. Since Jack and I were behind the tripwires looking out, I could barely see the daylight glinting off the thin metal lines. If we were walking the other way with the light at our backs, they'd be invisible. *Whew!*

Jack led the way, and the two of us carefully navigated through them, careful not to spring any traps.

"You'd think there'd be a way around these, "Jack grumbled, stepping cautiously over the last wire. "There's no way someone using this tunnel would take the time to dance through all of these ever time..."

I looked around. "Oh yeah," I said, noticing a tiny nook in the stone wall, disguised by the shadows. "Here's something." I got a closer look. Yep. "It's a little hidden passage—takes you right around." The tunnel was hidden in the wall. If you didn't know that it was there, it'd be really easy to pass on by.

Now we were close to the mine's entrance, I could see the backside of a huge waterfall.

"Hey, this looks like the same waterfall we saw running down into the ravine!" Jack said. "That means ... we're pretty close to the high road."

"Whooo!" I danced a little jig. "We're almost out of here, with the gold!"

"But how do we get out?" Jack asked, standing at the entrance and scanning the rocks. Infinite heavy water poured down in front of us, cascading over the tunnel's exit with a misty roar. I bent as close as I could to the fall, trying to see the rocks and everything around it. There didn't seem to be a way up or down, and you *definitely* couldn't go into the water. You'd be crushed on the rocks below...

"Let's look around," I suggested. "Maybe there's a hidden passage to the top somewhere."

We searched the tunnel for more secrets, but didn't find anything out of the ordinary, other than a weird stone archway in the wall that didn't go anywhere. A normal archway would have led into another area, but this one—on the other side of the stone-block archway—led to just a rocky wall. There was no torch holder; no levers or buttons. I looked over the stone wall itself...

"Jack, *look!*" I exclaimed, pointing to a chest-high rock next to the arch. There was a very faint 'A' carved into it.

Anderwyn, I thought. The world I saw on the enchanting table down below.

We looked at each other.

"What's it mean?" Jack asked. He pressed the rock, but nothing happened.

Dare I try? I had a feeling of what to do...

"I'll try it." I said, then I spoke loud and clearly. "Anderwyn."

Rock grinded against rock, and a door swung open. Both Jack and I crouched, ready to spring ouy of the way of a giant blade trap, or to dodge fireballs or something...

Nothing bad happened. Once the secret door was open, I saw a little landing on the other side, and a staircase leading up. Another staircase led down.

"Where'd that word come from?" Jack asked.

"I saw it inscribed on one of the enchanting tables, remember?"

"Oh yeah."

We stared at both stairways for a moment. It was quiet, aside from the roaring waterfall nearby.

"Seems okay," I said, then headed in and up, Jack following behind. I was very intrigued by where the lower stairs went to, but right now, I just wanted to get out and home.

Many rising flights later, then through a couple of long corridors, Jack and I were stopped by a block wall. We could see another 'A' in a stone.

"Andy when," Jack said proudly.

Nothing happened.

I smirked at him, then faced the *A*. "Anderwyn..."

A door noisily slid open.

We stepped outside into the sunshine, next to the old stone shelter by the river. The high road was within sight.

We were out!

Book 4, Chapter 5

The afternoon fresh air was a welcome thing. We'd been underground for one? Two? Three days? It was impossible to tell.

A moment after stepping outside, the door ground shut again. There was a faint 'A' in the middle of the closed door, but otherwise, it would be impossible to find if you didn't already know that it was there...

"Anderwyn," Jack said, looking at it. It opened again. "Nice," he said, voice full of admiration. "If you didn't know about the tricks, you'd run into tripwires, bug traps,

guardian hordes of skeletons and spiders—
and who knows what *other* defenses we
missed!?"

"Amazing," I said, taking a deep
breath and turning my face into the sun. I
wanted to know who this Anderwyn was
and what happened to him...

Jack turned to me and said, "I've
been thinking, Ru. We shouldn't tell anyone
about this cavern."

I nodded, "I was thinking the same
thing. It *is* special." The thought of hordes
of random people bumbling around in
there, stripping the cavern clean, and
stealing all the enchanted items made my
stomach hurt.

"I don't even want *Ralph* to know," Jack added. "I think he'd protect it, but ... just to be sure." Jack looked at me anxiously.

I held out my hand. "I'm with you, Jack. Let's protect the secret of this enchanted cavern. We can just say that we find the gold in some mine cart chests."

He nodded, and we shook hands. It was done.

"How about hiding all the enchanted stuff we took before saying goodbye to Ralph? We can pick it up again on the way back home," Jack said.

I nodded, then turned back to the door.

"Anderwyn."

The door opened again.

"Good idea," Jack said.

We stashed a couple of bags behind the secret door—including our fancy, new weapons—then waited to make sure the door sealed up again.

"Now let's get the horses and head home!" I exclaimed, leading the way to the high road.

It took a couple of hours walking to get back to the corral. By then, it was dark, but no creatures bothered us. I wasn't even worried. What were a few zombies or wolves after the day we'd had?

Silver heard me coming, and said *hello* with a loud neigh. Bucky and Blanco joined him in whinnying and stamping to welcome us back. There were torches lit throughout the structure, and it was a glorious sight; seeing our horses poke their fuzzy heads over the fence...

I ran up smiling.

"How are ya, fella?" I asked, rubbing Silver's forehead. "Sorry I don't have a sugar cube for you. Looks like Ralph was taking good care of you, though." My horse's coat was freshly brushed, and there troughs full of fresh water and food.

The stallion just bumped me gently with his forehead.

"Let's go say hi to Ralph," Jack said after he'd hugged Bucky and Blanco five times each.

Turned out the old man was waiting for us at the door of his massive mouse. "Come in, boys! Come in! I heard Silver announce your approach—how'd it go??" He clapped us on the shoulders, and from the way his curling mustache just about touched his eyeballs, it looked like he was grinning in happiness. "Come rest and eat!"

We followed Ralph inside. The fining hall table was set and waiting, so we didn't need any more encouragement. We excitedly stripped off our armor and boots, then plopped down at the table. Ralph served us hot mushroom soup to start with, and I've never tasted mushrooms any better!

"We got the gold we needed!" I exclaimed between wet, soupy bites. "Now I can save my parents! Thank you, Ralph. Thank you!"

The old man seemed genuinely happy for me.

"Tell me everything!" Ralph said. So we did. Mostly. Jack and I filled him in on a lot of the adventure. I let Jack take the lead in telling the tale, and Jack described getting lost, using the glowstones and how they helped, fighting cave spiders, and finding gold in chests. He mentioned *nothing* about the river, secret entrances, skeletons, or the cavern itself.

"It *is* a really dangerous place," I said finally. "If you don't mind, Ralph, we'll keep using the *fake* map. No one needs to go in there and get hurt..."

"Good idea," Ralph said. "Very good. But keep a copy of the *real* one, too. You never know when it might come in handy. Now ... how about a good night's sleep, and you two can be on your way first thing in the morning?"

Jack and I left at daybreak with Blanco loaded down with gold. The big white horse didn't even notice he was carrying extra weight.

Ralph stood at the corral waving. "Come back anytime, boys! But don't tell anyone about me!"

"Bye, Ralph! Thanks again!" I exclaimed.

Jack and I mounted our horses and rode away, out of sight, then stopped to pick up the enchanted things that we'd hidden. It was all still there, behind the magical door.

Now that I knew how to swim, I was a lot more confident around water. Instead of messing with the boat this time to cross the river, I just rode on Silver's back as the horses simply swam across. It was easy! And the high road was much easier going heading back than the way we had come up.

Eventually, we found ourselves emerging into Rabbit Valley, close to the shortcut path. Of course, you'd never see the path if you weren't looking for it. You had to weave in between three boulders, go through a narrow archway, and *bam!* There it was. Sneaky.

From Rabbit Valley with horses, we would be home that afternoon.

Finally! This crazy series of adventures was coming to a close!

In time, I looked down upon ... *home*.

As we approached my parents' house, Silver alerted his horse family with a high pitched whinny, and we galloped into town from there. I tried to have the horses walk into town in a dignified manner, but they wouldn't have it.

Silver and Bucky leapt the fence in one easy bound, making me cry out in surprise! That was the first time I'd ever jumped over something on a horse. It was fun!

Brew came running out of the shop followed closely by Smudge, who took one leap and landed on my head, purring madly.

"You're *back*, Ru! Hooray! How did it go? Did you get the gold? Oh, hi, Jack!"

I laughed and hugged my brother. "Yes. We found the gold. Will you help carry everything inside? Where's Bindr? He needs to make the *golden apples* now..."

Brew moved to pull a bag off of Blanco, then hesitated. "About Bindr, Ru..." His voice trailed off uncomfortably.

542

Oh no! I thought with a burst of fear. Had something happened to Bindr? Did he turn back into his evil, *witchy* self?

Jack and I stared at Brew.

"What happened?" I demanded.

"We don't know," Brew said. "Everything was fine. Bindr set up his things in the back room of the shop. He had a great time talking with Payj. Then, last night, he just up and dashed off with Pinto! There was no word; no explanation..."

"Pinto's gone too? Was Bindr's *skin* greener? He could have been turning into more of a witch, you know. It's happened before..."

Oh Blazes! What was Bindr up to, off on his own?

Brew walked us into the back room of the smithy. My brother had moved all the blacksmith supplies into a corner, and Bindr had reorganized everything *beautifully*, of course. Right in the middle of the room was a crafting table with another table next to it.

A pile of apples sat on the table, with an empty bushel beside them that was decorated with a little sign that said 'gold'. There was a book was on the table, opened to the instructions on how to craft golden apples. A note next to that gave instructions on how to change a zombie back into a villager.

"Did Bindr *expect* to leave?" I asked, full of amazement.

"I don't know." Brew said. "This area was like this yesterday when I went looking for him. But let's get our parents back first, and *then* we can worry about Bindr..."

"Yeah, okay," I said.

I was conflicted. Bindr was my friend, and I *knew in my heart* that he had to be in trouble, just like last time, when he tried on the black-gold armor and lost track of himself—turned evil—for a while.

But I had to save my parents. First things first.

I unloaded all the gold into its place next to the apples. It was a huge pile of gold.

"I think that's more than enough," Jack said.

"We should be able to rescue everyone in the village, and have some left over!" I said, almost happily.

Crafting golden apples was fun. We followed Bindr's directions to a T. We molded eight gold ingots around a single apple on the crafting table, compressing the gold in a way that I didn't understand at all, then a golden apple was made. Magical!

We did it many more times while Brew busied himself reading Bindr's notes on how to turn zombies back back into living people.

"It says to do it at night," Brew said at one point. "We need to put Mom and Dad in a little fenced enclosure so they can't hurt anyone. That makes a lot of sense. I'll go build a couple so that we're ready." He trotted off. I followed Brew to help him while Jack continued working with the gold and apples.

In time, we set up a sort of *transformation station*. I came up with the name, and the others liked it because it rhymed. When the time came to do the deed, we'd have to get the zombies—Mom and Dad, or any of the other villagers—inside and lock them in while have the ingredients ready and have plenty of light! Brew figured that we should also have a place for the newly turned villagers to sit down afterwards. And maybe a room for everyone to watch...

Brew and I were busy building our little structure when Payj the village librarian approached.

"Ru! You did it!" he exclaimed, clapping my armored shoulder.

"Payj!" I replied with a broad smile. "WE did it. Now we have to find out if all this *works*..."

Payj looked around worriedly. "Any sign of Bindr?"

I shook my head. "No, but he's probably okay." That was a lie, and I'm not sure why I said it. I *hoped* that Bindr was okay, but I had a bad feeling...

Brew and I walked Payj through the plan, and the younger librarian contributed some great suggestions on how to get the zombies *into the pen* as he called it. Then he, ran back to town to tell the rest of the village about what we were going to do.

A few hours later, it was nighttime.

Showtime.

All of our work, adventures, and challenges came down to this upcoming moment...

What if it didn't work?

The entire village turned out to watch. If this worked for my parents, it would work for *their* families too. I gathered up all of my strength and courage.

It was time to get Mom and Dad *into the pen*.

Brew and I went to the basement door, unlocked all of Brew's locks, then opened it slightly and stepped back. I heard the sound of zombie moaning coming from below, then crashing, and heavy footsteps shuffled up the stairs...

Cold fear flushed through me.

I was afraid to see Mom and Dad as zombies.

But I had to do this to save them. Brew and I needed our parents back. We needed to be a *family* again.

Brew and I had installed temporary fencing in the house to lead from the basement door to the zombie pens outside.

Now we just had to get our parents to emerge...

I stood in the temporary corridor like a carrot luring a pig.

"Mom, Dad. I'm home!" I called, trying to hide the tremble in my voice.

Mom came up first, her feet thudding up the stairs. As afraid as I was to see Mom green and decomposing, I was so happy to see her—I didn't even care if she was a zombie! Tears filled my eyes, and I almost ran to give her a hug.

"Ru!" Brew snapped, standing on the outside of the fencing, he pulled me back. "Come on!"

Oh right! I had to coax her into the pen. "Come on Mom. Come this way!" I walked backwards, and she shambled after me, her fingers now claws, stretched out to grab me...

Perfect!

Dad came out after her, and followed. It was sweet to see how they were still such a close couple!

We wanted to put my parents into separate pens. There was a slight concern that if one of them was cured, it wasn't immediately turned into a zombie again by the other. Brew had the great idea to use gates to block Dad as I closed Mom into her pen. Then we used the gates again to divert Dad into his own.

Getting my parents moved into their temporary holding cells worked like a charm.

Now for the cure...

"Mom or Dad first?" asked Brew.

"Dad," I said.

Brew looked at me, as if wondering why I decided as I did, then nodded.

Jack stood by, ready as a backup.

We were ready.

Brew splashed a *potion of weakness* on Dad. My zombie father immediately reached for us, groaning and snarling in a way that terrified me. I wasn't scared of zombies anymore—not when I knew that I could cut one to pieces with my sword. But I was horrified at the idea of having to destroy my father if this went wrong.

Little gray swirls surrounded Dad as the potion worked its magic...

I immediately reached into the pen and stuffed a golden apple into his growling mouth. Dad chomped down, probably thinking that he was eating my hand.

The swirls around my father turned to red. *Something was happening!* Dad started to shake and shudder. He moaned loudly, then his red eyes rolled up into his head...

We waited.

After a while—the entire village holding their breaths—I suddenly noticed the green of Dad's skin fading. It paled, then color rose until he was tan again. Once Dad's skin and hair was fully shifted back to normal, I watched in amazement as all of the scrapes, scratches, and bite-marks on the exposed parts of his face, neck, and body healed and smoothed over. His eyes rolled back, and I saw the green eyes of a living villager once again!

He made a noise. "Wha--?!" I realized that it was a word, and smiled, feeling tears roll down my face. "What's going on?" Dad asked. "What's everybody doing around me? What's happening?!"

Dad was cured.

A great cheer went up from the crowd.

Everyone was suddenly rushing around us, congratulating us, and clapping us on the shoulder. I ignored them all, and smiled from ear to ear, laughing loudly, letting my tears flow freely down my face. Brew was just as emotional. Jack laughed and smiled and wiped a tear away from one eye.

I turned toward mom.

"Everybody get back!" Jack shouted. "Come on, give them some room!"

Time for mom. Brew splashed her, and I stuffed a golden apple in her mouth, just like I did with Dad. After the same long episode of red swirls, shaking, and moaning, and I *finally* had my mom back as well!

I had never been so happy in my entire life!

"What am I doing in a pen?" Dad suddenly bellowed. "Brew! Ru! What have you boys been up to? Why is everyone staring at us?" Dad demanded, climbing over the fence. His face was red, but his eyes were confused.

Everyone laughed, then quieted down when my mom tried to speak.

"Ru?" she said, rubbing her head. "Are you wearing *armor?* You look very nice..."

"Ru's a warrior!" Brew exclaimed. "The *best* warrior!"

Mom suddenly screamed, and my heart leapt up into my throat.

"What's the matter???" I shouted, eyes wide and ready for anything.

"What are all these *horses* doing in my garden?!"

Everyone laughed, and I rushed forward to give her a huge hug. Throwing open the gate to her pen, I pulled her out and embraced her.

"Mom!" I replied, kissing the top of her head, "it's a long story!"

"Are we having a *party?*" she asked, hugging me back, looking around at the entire village in bewilderment.

Brew grabbed her and hugged her. "*Yes*, Mom! Yes, we are!"

It *was* a party. A celebration of *life!* Brew, Jack, and I spent the rest of the night changing our friends back into villagers, and the food and drink flowed freely as families were reunited.

Later, Brew and I sat with Mom and Dad, and gave them a short version of what happened. I figured that I would fill them in on the scary details of my adventures later.

Dad listened and watched me with astonishment. "*You?* Ru, you found a cure for us? You went to another village?" He broke down and cried. "My boy, I'm so sorry that I didn't want you to follow your heart and your spirit! You saved us, and I was totally wrong. I was to blame!"

Mom sat stunned and horrified throughout the tale. "I was a zombie? And I tried to eat my own children?"

"It's okay Mom! It wasn't you," I said, trying my best to console them of a big mess of guilt that was building up before my very eyes. "Dad, don't worry—it all turned out okay in the end. And now I'm stronger, and wiser, and I have many things to share with you."

Brew sat back and listened, impressed all the while.

I looked at my family and was filled with great love and pride. I had done it. I had fulfilled my oath.

562

"There's one major problem with all of this," Dad said, finally calming down.

Alarmed, I reacted quickly. "What? What's wrong?"

"Well," he said, glancing around the house, folding his big arms. "I know who I am, and I know that I'm a blacksmith. But ... I can't remember anything about *being* a blacksmith. It's like my skills have all been wiped—it's the strangest thing! What am I going to do?"

The big man wiped at his furrowed brown, lost and confused.

Brew spoke up with a smile. "Don't worry Dad. You taught me, now I'll teach you!"

Now that my parents were back to life, and things were going to be normal again—mostly—I still felt like there was more for me to do as a warrior. My oath to help my parents was finished, but I felt like something new and bigger was beginning...

There was a lot to do.

Jack and I had to find Bindr. I was sure that he was in trouble.

And there was a weird connection between the Blackened Knight and the zombie attacks. And his armor! That weird black-gold armor turned Bindr *evil*, and had a negative effect on Jack too. What was going on there? The Blackened Knight was involved with my village, and he was probably up to no good...

I knew I was destined to be a warrior, but so far, I had only learned the basics. I wanted to *train*—to really train. That was the only way to become a *great* warrior. I wondered if the Diamond Knight would have me as his apprentice, if I could find him...?

Soon, the sun would be rising. We were turning zombies and reconnecting with Mom and Dad all night!

I looked around as Mom and Dad and Brew chatted happily in the kitchen.

Smudge sat curled up on my lap, purring and sleeping.

Jack sat in an extra chair. He looked over at me and smiled, and I smiled back. He was my friend.

Eventually, I'd try to get some sleep in my bed again, for the first time in a long time.

I was looking forward to it—*blazes*, I was!

And I knew that I'd also be looking forward to the next adventure in the morning...

Wanna know what happens next??

Continue to the next book in series!

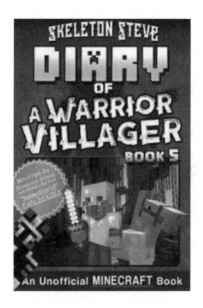

Love MINECRAFT? **Over 19,000 words of kid-friendly fun!**

This high-quality fan fiction fantasy diary book is for kids, teens, and nerdy grown-ups who love to read epic stories about their favorite game!

A Witchy Conspiracy

Ru is recognized as a mighty warrior, and his mom and dad have been healed of the zombie curse! Ru the warrior villager is recognized as a hero! So everything is great, right?? Well, not yet. Bindr--his witch friend--is still missing...

But when Jack and Ru go off looking for their missing friend, the trail leads into a very witchy swamp, and what they find there points the warrior villager and his friends to a nasty conspiracy involving kidnapped witches! Will Ru and Jack free Bindr? And what does the enslavement of the region's witches mean for Ru's village and his people?

CHECK OUT
SKELETONSTEVE.COM
... to find the NEXT BOOK!

Sign up for my Free Newsletter to get an *email* when the next book comes out!

Go to: **www.SkeletonSteve.com/sub**

Want More Ru and Friends?

1. Please go to where you bought this book and *leave a review!* It just takes a minute and it really helps!

2. Join my free *Skeleton Steve Club* and get an email when the next book comes out!

3. Look for your name under my *"Amazing Readers List"* at the end of the book, where I list my *all-star reviewers*. Heck—maybe I'll even use your name in a story if you want me to! (*Let me know in the review!*)

About the Author - Skeleton Steve

I am *Skeleton Steve*, author of *epic* unofficial Minecraft books. *Thanks for reading this book!*

My stories aren't your typical Minecraft junkfood for the brain. I work hard to design great plots and complex characters to take you for a roller coaster ride in their shoes! Er ... claws. Monster feet, maybe?

All of my stories written by (just) me are designed for all ages—kind of like the Harry Potter series—and they're twisting journeys of epic adventure! For something more light-hearted, check out my "Fan Series" books, which are collaborations between myself and my fans.

Smart kids will love these books! Teenagers and nerdy grown-ups will have a great time relating with the characters and the stories, getting swept up in the struggles of, say, a novice Enderman ninja (Elias), or the young and naïve creeper king

(Cth'ka), and even a chicken who refuses to be a zombie knight's battle steed!

I've been *all over* the Minecraft world of Diamodia (and others). As an adventurer and a writer at heart, I *always* chronicle my journeys, and I ask all of the friends I meet along the way to do the same.

Make sure to keep up with my books whenever I publish something new! If you want to know when new books come out, sign up for my mailing list and the *Skeleton Steve Club*. **It's free!**

Here's my website:
www.SkeletonSteve.com

You can also 'like' me on **Facebook**:
Facebook.com/SkeletonSteveMinecraft

And 'follow' me on **Twitter**:
Twitter.com/SkeletonSteveCo

And watch me on **Youtube**: (Check my website.)

"Subscribe" to my Mailing List and Get Free Updates!

I *love* bringing my Minecraft stories to readers like you, and I hope to one day put out over 100 stories! If you have a cool idea for a Minecraft story, please send me an email at *Steve@SkeletonSteve.com*, and I might make your idea into a real book. I promise I'll write back. :)

Other Books by Skeleton Steve
The "Noob Mob" Books

Books about individual mobs and their adventures becoming heroes of Diamodia.

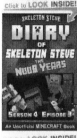

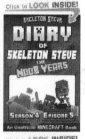

Diary of a Teenage Zombie Villager
Book 1 – *FREE!!*
Book 2
Book 3
Book 4

Diary of a Chicken Battle Steed
Book 1
Book 2
Book 3
Book 4

Diary of a Lone Wolf
Book 1
Book 2
Book 3
Book 4

Diary of an Enderman Ninja
Book 1 – *FREE!!*
Book 2
Book 3

Diary of a Separated Slime – Book 1

Diary of an Iron Golem Guardian – Book 1

The "Skull Kids" Books

A Continuing Diary about the Skull Kids, a group of world-hopping players

Diary of the Skull Kids
Book 1 – *FREE!!*
Book 2
Book 3

The "Fan Series" Books

Continuing Diary Series written by Skeleton Steve *and his fans!* Which one is your favorite?

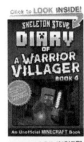  

Diary of a Warrior Villager
Book 1
Book 2
Book 3
Book 4
Book 5

Diary of Steve and the Wimpy Creeper
Book 1
Book 2
Book 3

Diary of Zombie Steve and Wimpy the Wolf
Book 1 *COMING SOON*

The "Tips and Tricks" Books

Handbooks for Serious Minecraft Players, revealing Secrets and Advice

Skeleton Steve's Secret Tricks and Tips

Skeleton Steve's Top 10 List of Rare Tips

Skeleton Steve's Guide to the
First 12 Things I Do in a New Game

Get these books as for FREE!

(**Visit www.SkeletonSteve.com to *learn more***)

Series Collections and Box Sets

Bundles of Skeleton Steve books from the Minecraft Universe. Entire Series in ONE BOOK.

Great Values! Usually 3-4 Books (sometimes more) for almost the price of one!

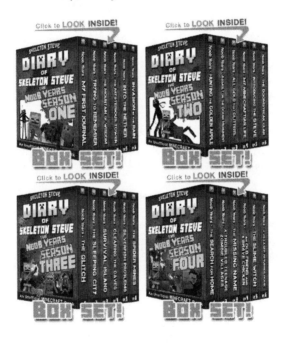

Skeleton Steve – The Noob Years – Season 1
Skeleton Steve – The Noob Years – Season 2
Skeleton Steve – The Noob Years – Season 3
Skeleton Steve – The Noob Years – Season 4

Diary of a Creeper King – Box Set 1
Diary of a Lone Wolf – Box Set 1
Diary of an Enderman NINJA – Box Set 1
Diary of the Skull Kids – Box Set 1
Steve and the Wimpy Creeper – Box Set 1
Diary of a Teenage Zombie Villager – Box Set 1
Diary of a Chicken Battle Steed – Box Set 1
Diary of a Warrior Village – Box Set 1

Sample Pack Bundles

Bundles of Skeleton Steve books from multiple series! New to Skeleton Steve? Check this out!

Great Values! Usually 3-4 Books (sometimes more) for almost the price of one!

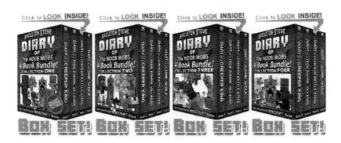

Skeleton Steve and the Noob Mobs Sampler Bundle
Book 1 Collection
Book 2 Collection
Book 3 Collection
Book 4 Collection

Check out the website
www.SkeletonSteve.com
for more!

Enjoy this Excerpt from...

"Diary of a **Lone Wolf**" Book 1

About the book:

Dakota was a young wolf, happy with his life in a wolf pack in the taiga forest where he was born.

Almost fully-grown, Dakota was fast and loved to run. He had friends, loved his mother, respected his alpha, and had a crush on a young female pack-mate.

But his life was about to change forever when his pack was attacked by *the Glitch*, a mysterious and invincible horde of mobs that appeared and started killing everything in their path!

Now, he was a **lone wolf**. With the help of Skeleton Steve, would he ever belong to another pack again? Would they escape *the Glitch* and warn the rest of Diamodia?

Love Minecraft adventure??

Read on for an Excerpt for the book!

Day 1

So how does a *wolf* tell a story? What should I say, Skeleton Steve?

Oh? Where should I start?

Okay.

So, I guess, my name is *Dakota*. I'm a wolf.

Heh … I already said that. I guess, technically, I'm a *dog* now. No? Doesn't matter?

Skeleton Steve is telling me that I'm a wolf. *Steve* calls me a dog. But I don't understand much about what *Steve* says.

Is this confusing? I'm sorry. Where was I?

Just from … okay, right before.

Well, I guess I can start by telling you about my old pack. My family.

Just a few days before the attack, it was a day like any other.

I woke up in the forest and leapt to my feet! It was a *beautiful* morning. The forest was in shadows of the rising sun, a cool breeze was crisp on my face, and I could smell the woods come alive! Approaching a tall pine tree, I scratched my shoulders on its bark.

All of my pack was waking up around me.

What a great life!

I ran down to the creek, and drank some water. Splashed my face into it. *Cold!* And shook my fur, sending drops of cold mountain water all over before bounding back up the hill.

I guess it's a good time to introduce *the pack*.

My eyes went first to the alpha and his mate. Logan and Moon. Logan was a huge wolf, and he was really nice. He and Moon didn't talk with us very much, but he was a good leader. Logan mostly kept to himself, quiet and strong, and he led us through the mountains day by day whenever we moved.

Right now, we'd spent the last several days hanging out *here*. There were fields full of sheep nearby, and with this nice, flat area, a mountain creek down the hill a bit, and plenty of shade, it was a good clearing to stay in for a while. I was sure we'd move on soon. We always did.

My belly rumbled. We didn't eat yesterday. Today, I knew the alpha would probably send Archie and me to scout out another herd of sheep for the pack to hunt. I was so *fast*, one of the fastest wolves in the pack, and Archie was pretty fast too, so Logan usually sent us out to find the food.

I loved my job! It was great, roaming around with my best bud, running as fast as we could, exploring the mountains all around the clearing where the pack lived. It was only last year when I was finally old enough to be given a job to do. I loved being able to help my family so well.

Taking a big breath of fresh air, I looked around at the rest of the pack waking up and frolicking in the brisk morning.

Over at the edge of the forest were Colin and Arnou. They were the *warriors*, really. We all help each other, and we all have shared tasks given to us by the alpha, but the big and muscular brothers, Colin and Arnou, were really great at fighting, and they were always the first to defend the pack against any mobs that attacked us—the first aside from *Logan the alpha*, that is.

There was my mother, Minsi, one of the older female wolves. I loved my mother. She sat on her own this morning, watching the birds and chewing on a bone.

Running and playing together was the mated pair, Boris and Leloo. Leloo helped raise the cubs (all of the females did, really), and Boris, along with his brother Rolf, were very good at hunting and taking down our prey. The two hunter brothers were very skilled at circling a herd of sheep or other food, and making the animals run whichever way they wanted.

Sitting in the shadow of a couple of pine trees were Maya, and her daughter, Lupe.

Lupe was my age.

She was a beautiful wolf. And smart too. And funny.

I dunno. For some reason, I had a really hard time *talking* to her. Archie joked with me a lot that I should make her my mate, but whenever I walked up to her, whenever I tried to talk to her, my tongue became stupid, I forgot was I wanted to say, and I just embarrassed myself whenever I tried.

It was terrible! Yes, I guess, I really, really liked her. It should have been easy!

Easy just like with Logan and Moon. Logan has been alpha since before I was born, but my mother told me that before he was alpha, when he was younger, he just walked up to Moon one day and *decided* that they were going to be mates.

I don't really understand how that works. Maybe one day I will.

"Hey, dude!" said Archie, running up to see me.

"Oh, hey! Good morning!" I said, sitting in the dirt.

Archie was a year older than me, and my best friend. When we were growing up, we always did everything together. And now that we were practically adult wolves (almost), we worked together whenever Logan gave us an assignment.

"You ready?" he said, wagging his tail.

"Ready for what?" I asked.

"Going to look for a herd, of course!" he replied.

"Well, yeah, but Logan hasn't told us to yet."

"I bet he will," Archie said.

Not an hour went by before the massive alpha called on us.

"Dakota! Archie!" he said, his deep voice clear above the rest of the pack, chatting in the morning. We ran up and sat before him.

"Yes, sir?" we said.

"You two explore down in the valley today, see if you can find another herd for us to hunt."

"Right away," I said. Archie acknowledged as well, and we departed our pack's temporary home, flying down the hill as quickly as our speedy wolf feet would take us. With the wind in my face, I dodged around trees, leapt over holes, exploded through the underbrush, and felt great!

When we emerged from the huge, pine forest, I felt the sun warm up my face, and I closed my eyes, lifting my snout up into the sky. Archie popped out of the woods next to me.

"Look at that," Archie said. "Have you ever seen anything so beautiful?"

The sunshine on our faces was very pleasant, and looking down, I could see a huge grassy field, full of red and yellow flowers. Little bunnies hopped around here and there, and in the distance was a group of sheep—mostly white, one grey, one black.

Beautiful. I thought of *Lupe*.

"Awesome," I said. "And hey—there's the sheep over there!"

We returned to the pack and led everyone through the forest back to the colorful and sunny meadow we found.

Soon, we were all working together to keep the sheep in a huddle while Logan, Boris, and Rolf, darted into the group of prey and eventually took them all down. After Logan and Moon had their fill, the rest of us were free to eat what we wanted.

I chomped down on the raw mutton and filled my belly. The sun was high, a gentle breeze blew through the meadow, and I felt warm and happy. Archie ate next to me, and I watched Lupe from afar, dreaming of a day when I would be brave enough to *decide* she was my mate.

Life was good.

Day 2

Today Archie and I went for a swim.

It wasn't necessary to go looking for more food yet, according to the alpha, so we were instructed to stay together, for the most part.

As a pack, we didn't eat every day. But sometimes, I got lucky and found a piece of rotten zombie flesh on the ground after the undead mobs burned up in the morning. Today wasn't one of those days, but it happened *sometimes*.

Anyway, it was fortunate that the mountain creek was just down the hill. Archie and I were able to run down and swim, while the rest of the pack sat around digesting all of the mutton we ate yesterday.

A section of the creek was nice and deep, so my friend and I splashed around and competed to see who could dog-paddle the longest. Archie won most of those times, but I know that I'm *faster* than him on the ground, ha ha.

There was a bit of a commotion around lunchtime when my mother happened upon a skeleton archer that was hiding in the shadows under a large pine tree. She gasped and back-pedaled as the undead creature raised his bow and started firing arrows into our midst.

Arnou was nearby, and responded immediately, with Colin close behind.

As the warrior wolves worked together to flank the skeleton, the mob did get *one* decent shot off, and Colin yelped as an arrow sank into his side. But the two strong wolves lashed out quickly, and were able to latch onto the skeleton's arms and legs, taking him down in no time. Only bones remained.

Colin and Arnou each took a bone, and went back to their business of lounging with the pack.

"Are you okay?" I said to my mother.

"Yes, thank you, Dakota," she said. "I'm glad you were out of the way."

"Oh come on, mom," I said. "I could have taken him."

"I know you could have, sweetie," she replied, and licked my face.

I don't know why the skeleton attacked. Sometimes the mobs attacked us. Sometimes not. Sometimes we (especially Colin and Arnou) attacked *them*. We did *love* zombie meat and skeleton bones, but I've never felt the urge to outright *attack* one of the undead to get it. I knew that if we were patient, we would always find more sheep and get plenty to eat.

Later that day, Archie caught me staring at Lupe, and decided to give me a hard time.

"You should go and *talk* to her, man!" he said, nudging me with his snout in her direction. Lupe noticed the movement, and looked over at us. I saw her beautiful, dark eyes for an instant, and then I turned away.

"Cut it out, man! Jeez!" I shoved him back with my body. "You made her look!"

"So what?" he said. "What's wrong with looking?" He laughed. "Maybe she *should* look. Then something will finally *happen*!"

I stole a glance back to her from the corner of my eye. She had looked away, and was laying in the grass again, looking at the clouds as they rolled by. Usually she hung out around her mother, Leloo, but she was by herself for the moment.

Could I? Did I dare?

"Look, dude," Archie said. "She's by herself. *Go for it!*"

I gulped, and looked back at my friend. I looked around at all of the other pack members. They weren't paying any attention. Just going about their own things.

Padding silently through the grass, I approached. Quiet. Well, not *too* quiet. Didn't want to look like I was sneaking up on her! I just didn't want to look *loud*. Okay, I needed to be a *little* louder.

Snap. Crunch. I made some random noises on the ground as I approached.

Jeez, I thought. *I'm being a total weirdo! What am I doing?*

Lupe turned her head to my approach, and when I saw her face, my heart fluttered.

"Hi, Dakota!" she said.

She was happy. Good. I wanted to see her happy. Make her happy. Umm ... if she *wanted* to be happy. Then I'd help her be happy. *What?*

"Oh ... hi," I said. Gulped.

She watched. Smiled. Waited patiently. What would I say? I couldn't really think of anything.

"How's it going?" she asked.

"Good. *Great!*" I said. "*Really* great!"

"That's cool," she replied.

I looked back, and saw Archie watching. He nudged at me with his nose from far away. *Go on*, he said without words.

"Uh," I said, "How are you?"

Lupe smiled and looked back at the clouds.

"Oh, I'm fine, thanks." Her tail gave a little wag.

"So, uh," I said, trying to think of something to talk about. "Did you get plenty of mutton yesterday? Lots to eat? I hope you ate a lot! *I mean*—not that it looks like you eat a lot, or too much. I mean—you're not *fat* or anything; I didn't think you look fat—"

Her face contorted in confusion.

Holy heck! What was I doing?

"Um ... I'm sorry! I'm not calling you fat I just ... uh ..."

Lupe laughed a nervous laugh.

"Ah ... yeah," she said. "I got plenty to eat. Thanks to *you*."

"Um ... me, and *Archie*. We found the sheep."

"Yeah, she said. "I know." She smiled, then watched the clouds.

"Yeah," I responded. I watched her, trying to think of something to say that wasn't completely *boneheaded*. After a few moments, she noticed me *staring*, and looked back at me. I looked up to the sky.

Her tail gave a small wag.

"Okay, well," I said, "I guess I'll go see how Archie is doing."

"Oh, really?" she asked. "Well, okay, I guess..."

"Okay," I said. "Well, bye."

"Bye," she said, gave me a smile, then looked back to the clouds she was watching.

I walked back to my friend feeling like an idiot, being careful not to walk like a weirdo.

Later that night, I laid in the grass, watching the stars. As the square moon moved across the sky, I looked at a thousand little pinpricks of light, shining and twinkling far, far away, drifting through space.

Most of the pack was already asleep. I could see Lupe sleeping next to her mom. Archie was sleeping near me, and the rest of the pack kept close together—my mother, the warriors and hunters, Leloo. The alphas slept away from us, a little ways up the hill.

The night was quiet, aside from the occasional zombie moan far in the distance, or the hissing of spiders climbing the trees. I was a little hungry, but tried to ignore my belly.

The stars all looked down at me from the vast, black sky, watching over all of us. So pretty.

Day 3

The morning started like all others.

We woke up and the pack was abuzz with hunger. It would be another scouting day for Archie and me. I ran down to the creek to splash cold water on my face, and found a piece of zombie flesh.

Even though I was hungry, I decided not to eat it. I took the delicious piece of meat in my mouth, careful not to sink my teeth into its sweet and smelly goodness, and brought it to my mom.

"Aw, *thanks*, honey!" she said. "Do you want to split it with me?"

"No, that's okay, mom. You have it," I said.

"But you're probably going to go looking for a herd with Archie today, right? You should take some and have the energy."

"That's alright, mom. I'll eat later."

"Okay, but I'll hang onto half of it in case you change your mind, okay?" She started to eat the zombie meat.

As we expected, Logan called on Archie and I to go out and find another herd of sheep. We happily complied, and ran through the forest for the better part of an hour, seeking out prey for the pack.

It was a warm day, and the breeze in my face felt great! My feet were fast, and the forest smelled good, and I ran like the wind. After a while, I caught the scent of mutton, and led Archie to a small herd of sheep wandering around in dense trees.

"There's our meal ticket!" Archie said. "Let's go back!"

"Let's *do it!*" I said, and we laughed as we sprinted through the woods back to the pack.

After dodging through the trees, leaping over boulders, and running silently through the straights like grey ghosts, we approached the forest clearing where the pack was living.

But something was *wrong*.

As we came down the hill, past enough trees to see the clearing, I smelled a weird smell. Something different that I hadn't smelled before. Something *alien*. And as we approached closer, I heard the sounds of battle!

Zombies moaned and growled. Skeletons clattered. Bows twanged, and arrows whistled through the air. I heard growls and scratches, thumps and crashes. Yelps and cries and raw wolf snarls!

"What the—?" Archie cried, as we ran down to the clearing.

Our pack was *fighting for their lives* against a group of zombies and skeletons!

I couldn't count how many of the undead were down there—the scene was confusing. For some reason, the battle was taking place in *broad daylight*, and the mobs weren't burning up in the sun!

In the chaos before us, I had a very hard time making out who was alive and who was already dead. The alpha was obviously still alive, running to and fro between the undead, striking with power and mainly pulling the attackers off of the other wolves. Moon, I think, was doing the same. Several wolves lay dead. My stomach suddenly turned cold...

CHECK OUT
SKELETONSTEVE.COM
... to CONTINUE READING!

Enjoy this Excerpt from...

"Diary of an **Enderman Ninja**" Book 1

About the book:

Love MINECRAFT? ****Over 16,000 words of kid-friendly fun!****

This high-quality fan fiction fantasy diary book is for **kids, teens, and nerdy grown-ups** who love to read *epic stories* about their favorite game!

Elias was a young Enderman. And he was a NINJA.

As an initiate of the Order of the Warping Fist, Elias is sent on a mission by his master to investigate the deaths of several Endermen at Nexus 426. Elias is excited to prove himself as a novice martial artist, but is a little nervous--he still hasn't figured out how to dodge arrows!

And now, when the young Enderman ninja discovers that the source of the problem is a trio of tough, experienced Minecraftian players, will he be in over his head? And what's this talk about a 'Skeleton King' and an army of undead?

Love Minecraft adventure??

Read on for an Excerpt for the book!

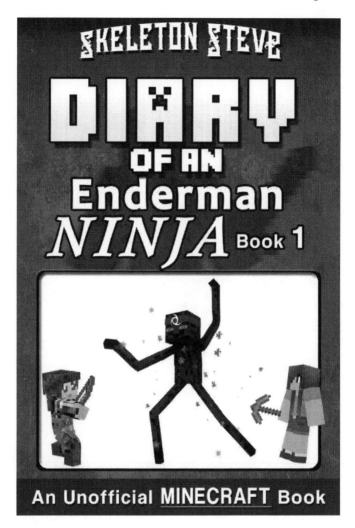

Day 1 - Overworld

When I teleported to the Overworld, I never thought that I would be starting a *diary*.

It is always interesting, the adventures that life puts in my path. So here I am, an Enderman, sitting on a rock and penning words into this empty book I found in a chest.

The day is clear today. Warm. Very pleasant.

It feels strange, trying to think of things to say with my fingers instead of with my mind, to use this archaic quill and ink to put words on paper.

The grass, and the leaves in the trees, are swaying and whispering in the wind, as I scratch these words onto paper in this leather-bound book resting on my lap.

Such is the way.

I am reminded frequently by the flow of the world around me to ignore my expectations, because once I expect something to go *one* way, the universe opens like a flower and teases me into another direction.

But I am ninja, so I flow like water.

Or, at least, I *try* to.

So I embrace this journal. This diary.

I will write of my adventures on my *Seed Stride*, and it will become part of my way. A painting of this path on my journey of life.

My name is Elias, and I am Ender.

I am also an initiate in the Order of the Warping Fist—a unique group of Endermen *ninja*. By now, I would have normally been granted the title of 'lower ninja', but the end of my initiate training was interrupted by the Seed Stride.

It occurs to me that writing this diary gives life to my story, and my story may travel on away from me once it has life. One day, my story and I may go separate ways—my body and my words separate, but together.

So I must explain.

The 'Seed Stride' is a rite of passage for young Endermen. Just before we reach adulthood and become full members of the Ender race, we are compelled to go on a Seed Stride. This is the first of many Seed Strides I will take over the course of my life, to help contribute to the well-being and expansion of my people.

We Ender, as a race, rely on the Pearls, our *Chi*, to produce more Ender, and to attune ourselves to the rhythm of the universe. Our Chi is also the source of our power to teleport, to warp between worlds, and also enhances our ability to communicate by the voice of the mind.

Such things we Ender take for granted. But it is possible that *you*, whoever picks up this book, as my story decides to *travel* later, may not understand the simple concepts that I've known since my birth.

So, now that you understand, *know* that my first Seed Stride was the reason my initiate ninja training was interrupted before completion.

Mature Endermen all understand, either through training or experience, how to dodge arrows and other missile weapons through the awareness they achieve by being in tune with their *Chi* and the world around them.

I'm still working on it.

When it was time to begin my Seed Stride, I was a little concerned that I hadn't yet mastered the Chi dodge, but as a ninja, I am comfortable enough in my combat ability to make up for my lack of skill in Chi.

Once my Seed Stride is complete, I will return to my master to complete my training. Then, I will increase in rank to lower ninja and start participating in real missions.

I understand that I am supposed to control my emotions. But the idea of finally being a real ninja and going on missions for the Order excites me! I'm sure that such excitement clouds my mind with impatience...

But I've got that impatience under control—really, I do!

So, I mentioned that the Ender people rely on the pearls. The pearls are the source of our enhanced power; the technology of our race.

I received my Ender pearl when I was very small. After going through the trials like all Ender younglings, I was chosen for the order. Some Endermen are more naturally in tune with their Chi than others. My connection and potential showed that I would be one of the few chosen to protect and further the race.

And now, I was almost fully-grown.

Though I recognize the value of humility, I was confident in my strengths.

I'm strong. And fast. And my martial arts skill is among the highest in my class.

I was sure that my connection with my Chi would catch up.

But I was out of time.

The time of my Seed Stride had come, so my training was paused, and now I am sitting on a rock in the sun, being one with the wind and the grass, and writing in this book...

Earlier today, I found a jungle.

The tall, green trees and lush ground was a most interesting biome! There were pools of water here and there, and I realized that a place so green had to experience frequent rain.

Warping through the environment, searching for pearl seeds in the dirt under thick vegetation, I knew that I needed to stay sharp—I wouldn't want to get caught in the rain!

But it didn't rain.

And I found *four* pearl seeds in dirt blocks during the time I traveled and warped through the interesting and lush environment. Trying to sense the Ender energy within, I picked up and discarded block after block of dirt until I could feel the pull of the Chi inside.

Whenever I found a dirt block containing a pearl seed, I opened my dimensional pocket, and stored the block with the other seed blocks for my return home.

The dirt blocks I collected would stay inside the dimensional pocket until I returned to the End at the completion of my Seed Stride.

There was no requirement or limit on the amount of blocks an Enderman was expected to collect on a Seed Stride. Finding the pearl seeds for our people was something engrained in us from an

Diary of a Warrior Villager
Book 1-4 - Ru's Adventure Begins!

early age—something we were expected to do as a service to our race.

I figured that I would know when I had collected enough seeds. My heart was open, and I would listen to my instinct. Once I finished this Seed Stride, and was satisfied with my service to the Ender people, I would return to the End to plant my seeds and continue my ninja training.

Some Endermen collected more seeds than others. And some dedicated their *entire lives* to the Seed Stride, walking the Overworld forever in search of the dirt blocks that held the promise of a growing pearl.

I would work hard, and collect many seeds. My life as a member of the Order was sworn to a duty to the people, after all. But my real goals lay in the path to becoming a better ninja.

I loved being a ninja. And once I rose to the rank of a lower ninja, I would at least have the respect of my peers.

Yes, maybe I suffered from a *little* bit of pride. I was aware.

But I knew what I wanted.

I wanted to be the best.

The strongest and fastest ninja. I wanted to be a shadow. In time, I hoped that I could even become a master, and be able to channel my Chi into fireballs, and do all of the other cool ninja stuff that Master Ee-Char could do.

So far, I had twenty-seven seeds. Pausing to peer into my dimensional pocket, I counted them again. Twenty-seven blocks of dirt, all holding the promise of growing an Ender pearl to be joined with twenty-seven Ender younglings in the future.

Perhaps one of them would also become a ninja, like me.

When I was in the jungle, earlier today, I found an old structure. Old for *Minecraftians*, I guess.

The small building was made of chiseled stone blocks, now overrun with vines and green moss.

As I explored the inside of the old Minecraftian structure, I noted that it was some sort of *temple*. My ninja awareness easily detected a couple of rotting, crude traps, and I avoided the trip lines and pressure plates without effort.

Inside a wooden chest, among a bunch of Minecraftian junk and zombie meat, I found *this book*.

Out of curiosity, I experimented with the levers by the stairs, until I revealed a hidden room with another wooden chest. Just more junk. Pieces of metal and bones.

Those Minecraftians and their junk...

At least, I *figured* it was Minecraftian junk. I had never personally *met* one of the creatures before. From what I'd heard in my training and tales from other Endermen, the Minecraftians were small and weak, but were intelligent, and were able to transform the Overworld into tools, armor, and other technology that made them stronger.

The older Endermen told me stories about the famous *Steve*, as well as other Minecraftians that came and went frequently on the Overworld. We even saw a Minecraftian or two appear every once and a while on the dragon's island, stuck on our world because of dabbling with portal technology they didn't understand. I've never seen them myself, but I've heard about the incidents from Endermen who were there at the time.

Usually, the visiting Minecraftians had it out for the dragon.

It never lasted long.

Apparently, they were usually surprised when they appeared on the obsidian receiver, and realized that there was no way to get home! I've heard that when they inevitably decide to attack the dragon, the great, ancient beast just *plucks them up* and throws them out into the void.

Well, now I had a piece of their junk. This book was constructed from leather and paper, which was likely constructed from something else. This ink was created by Minecraftians as well—all components derived from plants, animals, and minerals of the Overworld, to be sure.

What a beautiful day!

This Overworld is very bright during the day—uncomfortably so. But it's very peaceful and lovely.

I think I'll meditate for a while and write more tomorrow...

Day 2 - Overworld

After meditating, filling my Chi, and exploring the Overworld during the night, I decided to stay out in the open again during the next day.

I ran into another couple of Endermen during the night, a time when exploring is a lot easier on our eyes. But now, during the day, now that the sunlight is flooding the world around me, I'm all alone again.

During my training, I was never told to only go out at night, but it seems to be an unspoken rule of my people on the Seed Stride here. And I can understand why. The sun was so bright and hot on my eyes! But I didn't care. Let the others go into hiding or warp back to the End during the day. I had *seeds* to collect and an infinite world to explore!

Today, I observed the animals and the Overworld's native mobs.

There were several different kinds of beasts that I found, as I teleported from valley to valley, hillside to hillside, as the sky lightened with the rising sun. White, clucking birds, fluffy sheep, spotted cows, pink pigs. I was able to understand them by using my Chi to perceive their thoughts, but their language was very basic and they mostly communicated with each other through grunts and noises.

"*What is your name?*" I asked a particular chicken with my *mind voice*.

"*I am a chicken,*" it thought back. "Bawk!" it said aloud.

"What is your purpose?"

"I am eating."

The bird scratched at the ground with its goofy yellow feet, pulling plant seeds out of the tall grass.

As the morning went on, I noticed that some of the larger, more complicated creatures, the *mobs*, as I was taught they were called, *burst* into flames as the sun settled higher into the sky! Skeletons and zombies raced around, frantic and on fire, until they burned up and left behind nothing but piles of ash, bones, and charred meat.

What an interesting world.

As I teleported into the shadows of a tall, dark forest, I found a lone zombie hiding from the sun under a pine tree. He held a metal shovel in his hand—a Minecraftian tool.

"*Excuse me,*" I said into his mind.

"Who...? Who's there?" the zombie asked in a dull, slow voice. The creature looked around with black eyes.

I stepped out from the shadows to where it couldn't help but notice me. It's not like I was *trying* to hide before—I don't know how it didn't see me.

The zombie's face stretched in surprise. "Oh!" it cried. "You surprised me! So sneaky!" It settled down, paused, and stood vacant for a moment before speaking again. "What you want?"

"*I was wondering ... why does the sun sets zombies on fire?*" I said into its mind.

The zombie was shocked. "The sun sets zombies on *fire?!*" It was suddenly very aware of the sunlight just outside of the shadow of the tree, and the poor undead creature clutched at the pine's trunk to keep away from the light.

"*Elias,*" I suddenly heard in my mind. The voice of another Enderman. "*Behind you.*"

Turning, I saw, across a sunny valley, was an area of deep shadow under a cliff—probably a cave. Another Enderman stood inside. From here, I could see his eyes glowing purple in the dark, and I could barely make out the white symbol of the *Order of the Warping Fist* on his black headband.

Another ninja.

I left the zombie, teleporting across the valley to stand before the other Enderman.

"*What is it, sir?*" I asked. It was Erion, a lower ninja from the rank just above me. He had finished his initial training, and would now be expected to perform minor missions while still taking training from his master. His headband was black instead of blue (like mine), but still bore the white symbol of a novice.

Soon I would have a black headband like his.

"Elias, you have been summoned by Master Ee'char. He has ordered that you return to the Temple immediately."

"But ... my Seed Stride...?"

"Master Ee'char is aware that you are on Seed Stride. He has sent me to find you and ask you to return to him, still." Erion broke eye contact for a moment, and glared around at the sunny valley. *"What are you doing exploring during the day?"*

"Thank you, Erion. I'll return directly," I said into his mind.

The other Enderman ninja nodded, then disappeared with a *zip* and a brief shower of tiny, purple motes of light.

I turned, and noticed that the zombie I was talking to was gone. In front of the tree, outside of the shadow and in the sunlight, was a pile of charred meat ... and a shovel.

Huh.

What a strange world.

Teleporting around on a single world was easy. It was a lot like making a long jump—didn't require much energy, much of my *Chi*. I could overdo it, of course. If I warped around too much in too short a period of time, I would ... get tired, in a way. If my energy became too low, I would have to wait, or meditate for a while, until I had enough Chi to teleport again.

While exploring during my Seed Stride, the more I practiced harnessing my Chi for warping, the more I could do it without resting. I suppose there would come a time when teleporting on one world like I did here—hill to hill, place to place—would become as easy as blinking my eyes. In time.

But not yet. I still had to try. Still had to focus. And I could still get tired.

Teleporting was easier today than it was yesterday, though. With practice, I'd be able to warp more without resting and recharging my Chi—I was sure of it!

Jumping to another world was a different matter, however.

Going back and forth between the Overworld and the End was difficult, and required me to focus and have very strong Chi. The act needed *all* of my energy. And I'd probably need to recharge quite a bit before I could do it again.

So I sat on the cool stone in the shadow of the cave mouth, my legs crossed, my hands open and resting on my knees, receptive to the Overworld's Ender energy.

I meditated for a while, and let my thoughts dissipate. Focused only on my breathing, I willed my body to be a *receiver* for the energy of the world—the combined energy of all of the pearl seeds hidden in the blocks around me ... the energy of the world's core. It all funneled into me, moving up my arms, my legs, spiraling to my center ... to my *Chi*.

My Ender pearl was warm inside of me.

And I warped home.

CHECK OUT
SKELETONSTEVE.COM
... to CONTINUE READING!

CURRENTLY FREE!!

The Amazing Reader List

Thank you SO MUCH to these Readers and Reviewers! Your help in leaving reviews and spreading the word about my books is SO appreciated!

Awesome Reviewers:

MantisFang887 EpicDrago887

ScorpCraft SnailMMS WolfDFang

LegoWarrior70

Liam Burroughs

Ryan / Sean Gallagher

Habblie

Nirupam Bhagawati

Ethan MJC

Jacky6410 and Oscar

MasterMaker / Kale Aker

Cole

Kelly Nguyen

Ellesea & Ogmoe

K Mc / AlfieMcM

JenaLuv & Boogie

Han-Seon Choi

Danielle M

Oomab

So Cal Family

Daniel Geary Roberts

Jjtaup

Addidks / Creeperking987

D Guz / UltimateSword5

Diary of a Warrior Villager
Book 1-4 - Ru's Adventure Begins!

TJ

Xavier Edwards

DrTNT04

UltimateSword5

Mavslam

Ian / CKPA / BlazePlayz

Dana Hartley

Shaojing Li

Mitchell Adam Keith

Emmanuel Bellon

Melissa and Jacob Cross

Wyatt D and daughter

Jung Joo Lee

Dwduck and daughter

Yonael Yonas, the Creeper Tamer (Jesse)

Sarah Levy / shadowslayer1818

Pan

Phillip Wang / Jonathan55123

Ddudeboss

Hartley

Mitchell Adam Keith

L Stoltzman and sons

D4imond minc4rt

Bookworm_29

Tracie / Johnathan

Jeremyee49

Endra07 / Samuel Clemens

And, of course ... Herobrine

(More are added all the time! Since this is a print version of this book, check the eBook version of the latest books—or the website—to see if your name is in there!)